"Can we make love?"

Nicolette asked, "Is it illegal to be intimate before the wedding?"

"It's not illegal." Malik's lips brushed the corner of her mouth. "If it were, I'd change the law."

She shuddered against him. He held her in his thrall. He was powerful but he never used force. He didn't need to.

"You're trapped," he said, studying her lying beneath him. "My prisoner."

"So what are you going to do to me?"

His gaze settled on her mouth. "Make you talk."

THEPRINCESSBRIDES

For duty, for money…for passion!

Discover a new trilogy from rising star author
Jane Porter!

Meet the royals—the Ducasse family:
Chantal, Nicolette and Joelle. Step inside their
world and watch as three beautiful, independent
and very different princesses find their
own way to love and happiness.

Look for the next two titles in the series,
coming soon:

The Greek's Royal Mistress
(#2424)—October 2004

The Italian's Virgin Princess
(#2430)—November 2004

Available only from Harlequin Presents®

Jane Porter

THE SULTAN'S BOUGHT BRIDE

THE PRINCESS BRIDES

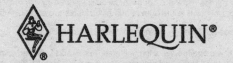

TORONTO • NEW YORK • LONDON
AMSTERDAM • PARIS • SYDNEY • HAMBURG
STOCKHOLM • ATHENS • TOKYO • MILAN • MADRID
PRAGUE • WARSAW • BUDAPEST • AUCKLAND

For C.J. Carmichael. Thank you for everything, Carla.
I am so very lucky to call you my
very good friend. Jane

ISBN 0-373-12418-X

THE SULTAN'S BOUGHT BRIDE

First North American Publication 2004.

www.eHarlequin.com

Printed in U.S.A.

PROLOGUE

"YOU'RE not going to go." Princess Nicolette tossed the heavy parchment paper into the garbage can. "You just pick up the phone and tell the sultan—or sheikh—or whatever he is that you're not doing this disgustingly barbaric arranged marriage thing again. For heaven's sake, Chantal, you're a woman—not a human sacrifice!"

Chantal's mouth curved, but the tight smile didn't touch her gray eyes, or her tense expression. "He's wealthy, Nic. There's a chance he might be able to buy Lilly's freedom, and if this is the way—"

"It's not the way! Absolutely not the way. You barely survived one hellish marriage. How could you even consider another?"

"Because our country needs it. Our people need it." Chantal's slim shoulders lifted, fell, as did her voice. "My daughter needs it."

Chantal's resignation killed Nic. Her sister had lost her spirit, her backbone, her courage. The last couple of years had virtually annihilated the elegant princess, the eldest of the Ducasse royal grandchildren.

"*You* have needs, too," Nic shot back. "And you need to be treated kindly, lovingly, with respect. Another marriage of convenience—to another playboy—will only crush you." Nic's emotions ran high. If Chantal couldn't fight anymore, then Nic would have to do it for her. "And I know you want to help Lilly, but your daughter needs to come home to Melio, Chantal. She doesn't need another foreign country, another foreign culture, or another foreign nanny saying *no princess, you can't princess, don't smile princess, we don't approve of laughter, princess!*"

Chantal winced. "You're not helping, Nic."

Nic dropped to her knees, and wrapped her arms around

Chantal's legs, holding her sister close. "So let me help. Let me do something for a change!"

Chantal's fine dark brown eyebrow arched and she lifted one of Nicolette's long blond curls. "You'll marry the sultan?" Chantal gently mocked. "Come on, Nic. You'd never agree to a marriage of convenience. And you're not even close to being ready to settle down. You're still sowing all your wild oats."

Nicolette pressed her cheek to Chantal's knees. "I'm not sowing wild oats. I'm just dating—"

Her sister laughed and tugged on the long blond curl. "You don't date, love. You hunt and destroy."

"You make me sound like the Terminator! I don't destroy men. I just haven't found Mr. Right yet."

"And how are you going to find the right man when you sleep with all the wrong ones?"

"I don't sleep with everybody."

"But you do like sex."

Nic eyed her sister thoughtfully. "Uh-oh, big sis doesn't approve."

"Big sis worries about AIDS. Venereal disease. Herpes. Pregnancy."

But that wasn't really what Chantal worried about, was it? Chantal wasn't thinking about Nicolette contracting a disease. She was worrying about her sister's reputation. "Is this where you make the Good Girls Don't speech?"

"Well, Mother's not here."

"Which probably makes you glad because Mother wasn't a Good Girl, either!"

Chantal stiffened. "Don't speak of Mother that way, and more importantly, you know we all need to make good marriages. This has been the plan for five years." Because their kingdom, consisting of two small islands in the Mediterranean Sea, Mejia and Melio, would be split at year's end. Mejia would revert to French rule, Melio to Spanish rule if the royal Ducasse family couldn't pay their taxes and trade agreements.

Chantal had been the one to suggest marriages of convenience. If the three princesses all made good marriages they could save Melio and Mejia, infusing the economy with new money, new alliances, new *power*. So Chantal had been the first to marry to Prince Armand Thibaudet of La Croix and it'd been a nightmare from the start.

So, no, Nic hadn't been overly anxious to marry, but that wasn't to say she wouldn't do her part. "You don't think I can marry well anymore, do you?"

If Chantal had heard the hurt in Nic's voice she gave no indication. "I don't know anything about your reputation, but I do know we all have a responsibility to take care of Melio. Succession depends on us. Melio's security, and stability, must come through us. We *are* the next generation."

"I've never shirked my duties. While you've been gone I've taken over your charities along with mine."

"Charities are all very well and nice, but it's money we need. *Millions* of dollars. And you have had two proposals, Nic."

"Years ago."

"Exactly! And nothing since. Because all the European royals know you've been voted by the press as the Ducasse princess least likely to settle down."

The criticism rang in Nicolette's ears. It still rankled Nic that Chantal continued to perceive duty...responsibility...as the best of personal virtues. "You're saying your sultan, King Nuri, would never propose to someone like me?"

"Well, he didn't, did he?"

Nic stared at Chantal for a long moment, realizing that even if duty-bound Chantal wanted to go to Baraka to meet the Sultan, Nic wouldn't let her. Chantal had been through too much in the past few years. No one but Nic knew about Chantal's private hell. Even Joelle, their youngest sister, knew little about the abuse Chantal suffered at the hands of her late husband.

"There's no reason for any of us to marry the sultan," Nic said after a moment. "We can get him to help us without giving up our freedom, and yes, I do value my freedom." Her gaze locked with Chantal's. "We'll get Lilly free. We'll bring her home."

Chantal shook her head. "Her grandparents will never let her go."

"They will if pressured properly." Nic's gaze held her sister's. "They will if King Nuri insists. You did say he was immensely powerful."

"And wealthy," Chantal whispered.

"So I'll go to King Nuri and ask for his help. He won't say no to his future bride, will he?"

"Nic—"

"I'll go, pretend to be you, get him to fall in love with me—"

"*Nic.*"

"He's a man, Chantal. I know how to manage men."

"It's not going to work. You'll never be able to pass yourself off as me. You're blond, I'm dark—"

"I'll dye my hair. As a brunette I could pass for you." Nic suddenly laughed, empowered. "I'll sneak in, sneak out. He won't even know what's happened."

"Oh, Nic, this is a disaster waiting to happen!"

"Not if I'm smart," she answered smugly. "Trust me. I can do this. I'll put together a plan, and you know me, Chantal. When I want something, I always win."

CHAPTER ONE

KING MALIK ROMAN NURI, sultan of Baraka, stood on the ancient harbor wall constructed nearly seven hundred years ago, in the shade of a sixteenth century Portuguese fortress and watched the royal Ducasse yacht sail into his harbor, ship's purple and gold banners flying high.

His princess was here.

His thick lashes lowered as he heard his band strike up a song of welcome, and he wondered at her thoughts, the thoughts of the beautiful Ducasse princess who'd left her home for his. Her world was Western, his was Eastern. She must feel some fear. He felt fear for her. She was coming to a world far different from her own. Her life would never be the same.

Did she even know it yet?

Standing on the gleaming wooden deck of the *Royal Star*, the Ducasse yacht named after Nic's late mother, Nicolette adjusted the long dark head covering she'd donned, and listened to the ship's flags snap in the hot afternoon wind, even as her own body crackled with tension.

She was determined. Focused. She knew what she had to do.

Her plan would work. There was no reason it shouldn't.

She'd arrive in Baraka, pretend to be Chantal, proceed with the wedding, and then once Chantal and Lilly were safe in America, the wedding would be called off.

Simple. Doable.

With her narrowed gaze on the horizon, the formidable stone walls of Atiq, Baraka's capital city, took shape. The fortified rampart facing the sea appeared to be centuries old, buffeted by storm and sea, and countless marauding neighbors. Nic could easily imagine those ruthless neighbors—The Greeks. The Romans. The Turks. The Portuguese. The French.

Everybody wanted to own something. If not a woman, then a piece of land. She could just picture the sailors, the soldiers,

9

the adventurers grabbing up chunks of soil and sand. Anything for power.

Nic stifled the wave of irritation. She had to be careful, needed to keep tight rein on her temper. She had to be charming, not angry. Sweet-tempered, not feisty. It was vital King Malik Nuri believe she was really Chantal.

Pulling the head scarf closer to her face, concealing her mouth and nose, she drew a deep breath and chased away all thoughts of conquerors and kings. Instead she studied the looming port with the dots of green palm trees shadowing the glaring white walls of the inner city.

For a moment, Nic's curiosity upstaged her emotions. Was this where she'd stay during the next couple of weeks? Did the sultan live in the harbor city of Atiq? Or was his palace elsewhere…perhaps tucked inland, protected by the massive dunes of the Sahara?

And as her gaze focused on the distant horizon, music wafted over the water. She spotted the enormous crowd gathered on the rampart walls. Hundreds and hundreds of people waited for her.

So much for sneaking in and out.

Beneath Nic's long robe, something she'd cheerfully put on as it aided her disguise, her toes curled inside her sleek leather pumps, the shoes matching her hidden lavender silk suit perfectly, the suit vintage designer—something from her mother's collection, and she shook her head at Chantal's choices all over again.

Why on earth would someone like King Malik Roman Nuri choose Chantal for his bride? And why on earth would Chantal even consider saying yes to yet another unfaithful husband?

Nic had spent all last week on the Internet, poring over media archives. She'd done her research and she knew King Malik Roman Nuri for what he was. A handsome, but irredeemable playboy.

From the few grainy photos she'd been able to pull up, he was certainly attractive. He had hard, masculine features, a thick head of hair, and apparently a stunning libido.

The gossip magazines claimed the sultan, Malik Nuri, was The Casanova of Arabia. According to several sources close to the sultan, King Nuri had mastered seduction, turned lovemaking into an art, and kept numerous mistresses—all in splendid style.

Fine. He was a world-class lover. He spoile
After Chantal's experience with one manipulativ
husband, she certainly didn't need another who'd
vows of fidelity, much less loyalty.

Nic grit her teeth. Chantal deserved a prince of ɒ man, not a
sultan unable to keep his royal trousers on!

The band's bright notes jarred her, even as they filled the air.
Two weeks, three weeks, she told herself, fighting her temper,
not a day more. They'd leave for the United States as soon as
it could be arranged. She'd propose a wedding in her mother's
home town, something very small and private, yet meaningful,
and once they were in Baton Rouge, Nic would call the wedding
off.

If she handled this right—flattering the sultan, giving him the
kind of attention she knew how to give a man—the whole charade would be nothing but a feminine escapade. The engagement
would be short. Sweet. *Painless.*

"Your Highness?" The ship's captain had appeared at her
side. "We have arrived."

Nic turned to the captain, a man she'd known nearly half her
life. He'd aged in the past decade, but then hadn't they all? And
he didn't know what she knew: this would be his last voyage
as captain of the *Royal Star*. The *Royal Star* was being put up
for auction on the ship's return to Melio. "Excellent."

"We've just about moored, Your Highness. Are you ready to
disembark?"

"Yes." And then she swallowed around the fierce lump in
her throat as she looked up into Captain Anderson's weathered
face, the creases at his eyes deep from years of squinting against
the sun. "And may I thank you for your years of loyal service,
Captain? You've been truly magnificent."

"It's been my pleasure, Your Highness." He bowed. "We'll
see you on your return home."

With the stringed instruments plucking, drums and tambou-
rines beating, Nic stepped onto the gangway and halfway across,
colorful confetti streamed down. It wasn't paper confetti, the bits
of orange and red and pink were flower petals and the sweet
scented petals drifted onto her covered head and shoulders.

It was like entering a dream world—the music, the colors, the

...t of spice in the air. Nic had the strongest sensation that this new world would soon dazzle her with its exotic secrets.

By the time she reached the end of the gangway, time had slowed. Faces blurred. People were cheering and clapping but none of it sounded real. The language was different, the faces weren't familiar, there was nothing here that resembled the life she'd known.

Her gaze searched the crowd, trying to find a landmark...a personal touchstone. She found none. Instead the heat beat at her, hot and humid and oppressive, and the noise rang in her ears, too loud, too insistent, and for a half second everything swam before her eyes, a blur of orange and crimson, sharp, discordant sound, and she blinked once, trying to clear her head, trying to find herself again.

Nic gripped the gangway railing and tried not to dwell on the fact that she, Tough Girl, was suffering from a case of nerves. Focus, she lectured herself. Find a face in the crowd. Get your legs under you. Pull yourself together.

And she did.

She found a remarkable face in the crowd. It belonged to a man of course, she'd always had a soft spot for the opposite sex, and this man certainly caught her interest, quickened her pulse.

Arresting, was the first word that came to mind. Darkly arresting. She liked his strong hard face with the dark sunglasses, the thick black hair which framed his wide brow. She even liked the way he wore his sophisticated dark suit, with his crisp white shirt open at the collar.

He looked cool, calm, different from the others.

Her gaze clung to him, grateful for the normalcy. No robes, no camel, no chanting from him.

Good.

His sunglasses shaded his eyes and added to his mystique. She tried to imagine what his eyes would be like. Dark? Sable brown? Golden, perhaps?

It really didn't matter, not with that thick, slightly wavy hair, and a face that made her think of lips...kisses. His jaw was as broad as his brow, his nose rather long but his lips curved faintly. They were *very* nice lips.

Then he pulled off his sunglasses and she inhaled a little,

intrigued by his expression. It was arrogant. Proud. Challenging. He looked like a man who enjoyed a good fight. Interesting. She enjoyed a good fight, too.

Nothing turned her on as much as a man wrestling with her, rolling her beneath him, pinning her hands to the bed.

Mmm, it'd been too long. Too bad they weren't in Melio. What she wouldn't give for a night alone with him. She'd like to test his pride as well as taste his intensity. He'd be great fun on board the *Royal Star*, or for a night playing in nearby Monte Carlo, but there was no way anything was going to happen here. She was Chantal, she reminded herself, ending the brief fantasy, and she was in Baraka to discuss a wedding.

Conscious of a thousand pair of eyes resting on her, cymbals still clanging in her ears, Nic wished the sultan would step forward and get the introductions over.

For a moment no one moved, then a small, very stout robed man with dark mustache and beard moved toward her.

"Princess Chantal Marie Ducasse?"

The man barely reached her shoulder. Nic was tall, taller than either of her sisters, but this man would have been short standing next to even them. "Yes."

He bowed. "May I present to you, His Royal Highness, King Malik Roman Nuri, sultan of Baraka, prince of Atiq."

The crowd shifted expectantly and their tension sent arrows of dread straight through her middle. For a half second she regretted agreeing to this, wishing she'd stayed comfortable and ignorant at home.

Then she straightened her shoulders and the front row of the crowd opened, allowing a tall man in a dark suit to pass through. *Him.*

No, she silently cried, not *him.* Anyone but him. But he was moving toward her, slowly, languidly, and her legs went weak.

This was not a good thing.

She swallowed, tried to see past his sunglasses which were again hiding his gaze, but instead looked at his mouth. The mouth that had made her think of lips, and kissing and…sex.

Her mouth dried. She suppressed a wave of horror. She'd seen the Sultan's picture on the Internet and she wracked her brain, trying to put together the grainy photos with this man but it didn't fit. She'd imagined a shorter man, heavier set, easily managed and rather spoiled...

This man didn't look easily managed at all.

"His Royal Highness," the short man intoned with a deep bow.

Her heart thudded, turned over, and her legs felt quivery. "Your Highness?" she murmured, hearing the doubt in her own voice.

The sultan closed the distance between them and studied her for a long silent moment. Nicolette was the first to look away, glancing down to the ground to hide her confusion.

But the Sultan wouldn't let her escape. He tilted her chin up with his fingers, again gazed down into her face, and then apparently satisfied, he kissed her on each cheek.

"*S-salamu alikum,*" he said soberly, his voice so deep she had to strain to hear him.

"Peace on you," the short man translated with another bow. "His Highness welcomes you to his beloved Baraka. Land of a thousand dreams."

Land of a thousand dreams. Interesting. And rather provocative, too.

"Thank you," she murmured, her cheeks still hot from the brush of his lips, and her brain racing to assimilate everything she was learning—such as the fact that the sultan didn't speak English. "Would you please tell His Highness that I am flattered by the warm welcome his people have given me?"

The translator passed the message on before turning back to Nicolette. "His Highness thinks it would be good to get you out of the sun. His car is waiting just there," and he pointed to a dark limousine behind them, surrounded by uniformed guards.

The translator sat on one long seat in the limousine while Nicolette and the silent sultan sat on the other.

She and King Nuri didn't speak during the brief drive, and although he barely looked at her, Nic had never felt so uncomfortably aware of anyone before.

She was conscious of the way he sat, feet planted, knees parted, thigh muscles honed. She felt the way he breathed—slow, deep breaths as if he owned the very air. His fragrance was light and yet the faint hint of spice made her want more.

He shifted abruptly, his arm extending on the back of the

black leather upholstery seat, his hand precariously near her shoulder. Nic shimmered with sudden heat, her skin prickling all over. She felt each fine hair on her nape rise, and her nipples tighten.

Bizarre. Impossible. She hadn't responded to a man this strong since…since…

She shook her head, not wanting to go there. It was bad enough trying to cope with her dazed senses without throwing memories of Daniel into the mix.

"Your luggage will follow," the translator volunteered after a few tense minutes. "But if there is anything you require before your luggage arrives, you need only ask."

Nic nodded jerkily, grateful for the protective head scarf, knowing her cheeks were as hot as the rest of her. "Thank you."

They reached the outer gates of the palace, and Nic discovered the sultan's palace was actually a modernized fort, although to Nic's mind, the huge and richly embellished main gate seemed more suitable for decoration than defense.

Once inside the ornate gate, a miniature city appeared, gardens, courtyards, white stone buildings each elegant and unique, nearly all fronted by endless white marble columns.

Guards in white trousers, white shirts, black boots and white robes bowed as King Nuri led Nicolette and the translator across the central courtyard to the central building. The building they entered was larger than the others and the facade grander, but the large carved doors failed to hint at the grandeur inside.

The great doors were gilded, and in the interior the ceiling soared, at least two stories in height, every surface covered in gold, mosaic murals, and bronze detailing. Gold, treasure, and impossible beauty.

Awed, Nicolette followed King Nuri into an elegant salon, rich crimson carpets covered the marble floor. The King gestured to one of the low couches in the middle of the room.

Nicolette gratefully sank down on the edge of one couch, the cushion covered in stunning ruby silk, cocooned by the luxury and elegance.

"Refreshments?" the translator offered as a serving girl entered with a silver tray.

The smell of dark rich fragrant coffee made Nic's mouth water. She'd never needed fortifying as much as she did now. "Please."

Still standing, King Nuri gazed at Nicolette with unnerving focus. Then he broke the silence, and when he spoke, his voice was so deep and smooth that his words sounded like honeyed candy.

The translator explained the sultan's words. "His Highness trusts your journey was safe."

She nodded, forcing a calm smile. "Yes, thank you."

"No problems on your journey?" The sultan added.

Nic listened to the sultan's voice in her head, lingering over his syllables. He had the most unusual voice. Deep. Husky. Again her pulse lurched, her heart finding it hard to settle into a steady rhythm. "The trip was uneventful," she answered, knowing she'd better find her footing fast. If she couldn't control her response to him, how could she possibly control *him?*

"Hamadullah," King Nuri answered, the corner of his mouth curved in a small private smile.

She forced her attention away from the Sultan's lovely mouth. Remember his stream of mistresses, she told herself. Remember his reputation. "What does *hamadullah* mean?"

"It means, 'Thanks be to God'."

Nic mulled over the King's response.

King Nuri spoke again, and the translator hastened to explain. "It is customary here to express gratitude to God for our blessings."

Nic shot King Nuri a quick glance. His lips curved fractionally. Hollows appeared beneath his strong cheekbones. "And my arrival is a blessing?"

"Without a doubt." The translator answered, speaking for the sultan.

She shot King Nuri yet another wary glance. She'd thought she was prepared for this trip, thought her plan was bullet proof, but now that she was here, and he was here, and they were together…this wasn't at all how she'd imagined it. She'd pictured him rakish. Handsome but a little thick in the jowls, a little paunchy at the waist. She'd told herself he'd flirt outrageously, come on too strong, and probably wear flashy clothes, but that wasn't the man facing her now.

The sultan took a seat close to her on one of the low couches.

When he reached for his coffee, his long arm nearly brushed her knee and she shivered inwardly, tensing all over again.

Had she hoped he'd touch her?

Had she feared he'd touch her?

The sultan was speaking Arabic again, and Nic glanced from King Nuri to the translator and back. The King's profile was beautiful. He was beautiful. Definitively male.

"His Highness expresses his satisfaction that you are here. He says that he and his people have waited a very long time for this day."

Nic's fingers tightened around her small espresso cup, trying to keep her calm. The King was practically reclining, and his eyes, a cool silvery green-gray, rested on her as if he found her absolutely fascinating.

Thank God Chantal wasn't here. King Nuri would have seduced her, married her, and abandoned her in no time. If he was a man who lived off his conquests, then Chantal, so broken by marriage and life, wouldn't be enough of a conquest.

"I look forward to getting to know His Highness," Nic said in her most careful diction. "And to discussing my ideas for the wedding."

"*Your* ideas?" The interpreter asked.

Nic couldn't hide her impatience. "Yes. Of course. It's my wedding. I have ideas about *my* wedding."

No one spoke for a moment, and King Nuri's dark head tipped, his black lashes dropped as he studied her. His cool gaze examined her face, taking in each feature, the curve of bone, the very shape and texture of her lips.

The translator expressed her thoughts to King Nuri.

Then the sultan spoke, and the translator turned to her. "The king understands that you have just arrived, and everything feels quite new and alien, but he also asks you to trust him with the wedding details so they will comply with his beliefs and our customs."

"Please tell His Highness that I'd like to trust him with the wedding details, but a wedding is quite a personal event, and I insist I be part of planning it."

"The king thanks you for your concerns, and assures you that you need not worry, or be troubled. As the wedding details are set, there is nothing for you to do in the next two weeks but relax and familiarize yourself with our life here in Baraka.''

Nothing to do in the next two weeks but relax? Nic puzzled over the king's answer. "What's happening in two weeks?"

The translator bowed his head. "The wedding, Your Highness.''

The wedding already planned. The ceremony here. In two weeks. It couldn't be. Surely this was a language problem, an issue with the translation. "I'm afraid we're losing something here. Are you telling me that the wedding date—and all the detail—has already been set?"

"Yes."

Nicolette touched the tip of her tongue to her upper lip. She'd been in Baraka, King Malik Nuri's North African kingdom, less than two hours and already things were wildly out of control. What had happened to *her* plan? What about the quiet, private ceremony she'd dreamed up in America? "How can it be *set?*"

The robed translator bowed his head politely. "His Highness has chosen a date blessed by the religious and cultural calendar.''

Nicolette glanced past the stout translator to King Nuri reclining on the sofa. This was going to be far more difficult than she'd anticipated. King Nuri was the kind of man she'd assiduously avoided—smart, suave, sophisticated—and far too much in control. "But the king hasn't consulted my calendar," she said firmly, turning toward the sultan, meeting his gaze directly to convey her displeasure. "He can't set a wedding date without my input.''

The translator nodded again, his expression grave, and still unfailingly polite. "It is customary for the king to consult with his spiritual advisors.''

"The king is very religious then?"

The translator paused, appeared momentarily at a loss for words before recovering. "The king is the king. The ruler of Baraka—''

What nonsense was this? "And I am Princess Chantal, of the royal Ducasse family." Her temper was getting the best of her. She hated double-speak, especially hated royal double-speak. This is one reason she'd always dated commoners. *Playboys,* her sister's voice echoed in her head. "Perhaps you'd care to remind your king that nothing is set until I say it's set.''

The translator hesitated. He didn't want to translate this.

Nicolette's jaw hardened. "Tell him. *Please.*"

"Your Highness—" the translator protested.

She shifted impatiently, set her cup on the low wood table. "Perhaps it was a mistake coming to Baraka. I'd assumed King Malik Nuri was educated. Civilized—"

"Western?" the king concluded, languidly rising from his sofa to again dominate the royal chamber.

Nic's jaw dropped even as her stomach flipped.

So he spoke English. But of course he spoke English. She'd discovered on the Internet that he'd gone to Oxford for heaven's sake. Yet he'd allowed all introductions, all awkward conversation, to be made via the translator. He'd had their first meeting conducted like an interview.

"Why did we have a translator?" she demanded, head tilting, scarf sliding back, revealing her long dark hair.

He didn't look a bit apologetic. "I thought it might make you more comfortable."

Wrong. It was to make him more comfortable. A passive display of power. Nic scraped her teeth together. Think like Chantal, she reminded herself. Be Chantal.

But Chantal's become a doormat.

And yet it's Chantal he wants, not you.

The sultan was waiting for her to speak. Her eyes flashed fire even as she struggled to retain her flimsy smile, nodding her head the way she'd seen Chantal nod graciously so many times on official state business. "How considerate," she said from between clenched teeth, rising as well. "I really ought to…thank you."

King Nuri's lips curved faintly. "My pleasure." He lifted his hand in a small imperial gesture and the translator discreetly exited the room.

They were both standing, far too close for Nic's comfort, and the sultan studied her fierce expression for a long moment before knotting his hands behind his back and slowly circling her.

It was an examination. A study before a purchase.

Like a camel at an open-air market, she thought uneasily, as he circled a second time, his hawklike gaze missing nothing.

"Do I meet your approval, King Nuri?" She choked, her

sarcasm lost as her voice broke. This was not going to be a two-week vacation. She was scared. Not for Chantal, but for herself. King Nuri had a plan, and as the wild beating of her heart reminded her, his plan was swiftly annihilating her own.

CHAPTER TWO

THE king continued his examination, coming round full circle a second time before stopping in front of her, just inches away.

Nic held her breath, fighting for poise, trying not to blink or flinch but keep all responses hidden even though he did something crazy to her senses. Her head swam and her pulse quickened and right now she found herself fascinated by a dozen little things like the line of his jaw, the shadow of his beard, the deep hollow at his throat—

"You're taller than I expected," he said, breaking the taut silence.

She'd inherited her father's height, as well as his blond hair, and her height had been a problem for a lot of men, "So are you."

His eyes narrowed thoughtfully. "Your coloring is a little off, too." He shrugged. "But then I suppose people always look different on television."

"You *are* disappointed."

One of his flat black eyebrows lifted. "Did I say that?"

Nic's temper flared yet again, and she didn't understand it. Normally men didn't trouble her. Men didn't upset her. She was usually so adept at handling them. She understood the way they thought, the things they wanted, how best to soothe their fragile, ruffled egos. But the sultan didn't appear fragile, or egotistical, and so far, she hadn't a clue how to deal with him.

Malik calmly met Nicolette's furious blue gaze.

The princess had cheekbones and an attitude, he thought, smiling faintly. He didn't know why it made him smile. The attitude he'd expected—she was one of the beautiful Ducasse sisters after all—but the cheekbones intrigued him. In the princess the cheekbones were sculptural, architectural. Something one wanted to touch, trace, caress.

She'd only just arrived and yet he wanted to take her face in

21

his hands and stroke the sensuous curve of cheekbone that stretched from her hairline to just above her full mouth.

But then, she didn't just have cheekbones. She had lips, too. Lovely, full lips and wide winged eyebrows that reminded him of two birds flying free.

Where was the restrained regal face of Chantal? This wasn't the face of a gentle princess. The face before him had an edge of sensuality, and fierceness. He had no doubt that this woman could be strong, very strong, and he'd be a fool to let her long soft curls and soft full lips tell him otherwise. He knew from his own mother that the most delicate beauties could hide a tiger's heart.

"Did you bring no one with you?" he asked, breaking the tension. "No secretary or valet? No one to handle your social calendar?"

Nic shrugged. "I didn't think it necessary, Your Highness. I have cleared my calendar, made myself completely available to you."

"How thoughtful."

"I try," she said demurely, bowing her head, missing Malik's speculative expression.

She was up to something, he thought, looking at her bent head, her dark brown hair shiny, silky. Her hair was long and she wore it pulled in a low, loose ponytail. The style flattered her high cheekbones but somehow did little to soften her strong jaw. She had a firm jaw and chin for a woman. She was a woman accustomed to getting her way.

"But of course you need help," he said after a moment, knowing why she'd traveled alone, and understanding it had little to do with the Ducasse family's strained finances. It wasn't that she couldn't afford help. He guessed she wanted to be incognito. She didn't want any familiar staff assisting her.

The princess, he thought, was playing a game.

"Since you weren't able to bring anyone from home, I'm happy to provide staff for you," he offered sympathetically. "I have a few people in mind, and all have undergone rigorous training as well as a thorough screening for security."

The deepness, the richness of his voice still sent little shock waves through her. Nic felt the tremors on the inside, wondered how any man's voice could be so husky. "I don't really need a staff, Your Highness."

He brushed aside her protest. "You have a very busy schedule, Princess. You have many functions, and many activities planned. It is vital you have help organizing your calendar, as well as your wardrobe."

She blushed. She'd never been serious about fashion, and the few smart pieces she had were gifts from various French and Italian designers. "I brought very little in the way of wardrobe." Her polished smile hid her inner turmoil. He was not going to be easy to negotiate with. "I thought this was just a preliminary visit. Get acquainted, set the date—"

He thrust his hands into his trouser pockets, looking alarmingly Western. "But of course the date is set. We discussed this—"

"No, Your Highness, we never discussed this. You might have suggested a short engagement, but no date was ever set." She loved that she could be firm. No one had ever been able to bully her. "I would have remembered."

He gestured casually, and shrugged. "Regardless, I think two weeks is sufficient time, considering the fact that we both are anxious to move forward with our lives. One of the first staff members you'll meet is your wedding planner—"

"Two week engagement?" she interrupted, torn between laughter and indignation. Two week engagement for a princess? "It is impossible to prepare for a wedding in fourteen days."

"It's two weeks from Saturday which makes it eighteen days."

The issue wasn't fourteen days or eighteen days. The issue was not getting married…or at least, not getting married *his* way. If he wanted a wedding, she'd give him a wedding, she just wasn't about to be a bride, trapped in Baraka. "I have thoughts on the wedding, Your Highness. I've made some preliminary arrangements of my own."

"You have?"

"Yes. As my mother was American, I thought we'd fly to the States for the actual wedding." She saw his incredulous expression and hurried on. "I'd hoped to marry in my mother's parish church, just outside Baton Rouge, Louisiana."

His jaw tightened. "I've never even been to Louisiana. Have you?"

"No, which is why I want to go. I'd like my mother's family to be able to attend—"

"They can attend the wedding here."

"They're—" she swallowed hard, "—poor, Your Highness. Most have never been outside their county, much less on an airplane to a foreign country."

"So we'll send my jet. Problem solved." The Sultan walked to a bureau hugging a far wall, retrieved something from the top drawer and returned to her side. "Your schedule," he continued, handing her an appointment calendar. "As you can see, you'll be quite busy helping plan and prepare for the wedding here. Some things you'll do on your own. Many things we'll do together—"

"King Nuri," she interrupted, fingers burning from the brief touch of their hands, "forgive me for being obtuse, but I don't understand why we can't at least discuss my ideas for the wedding."

He lifted his head, met her gaze, his cool silver gaze still. "But of course we can discuss your ideas," he said after a moment. "I think its essential to incorporate as many of your family traditions into our ceremony here. This is exactly what I wish you to tell your wedding planner. You'll be meeting with her later today—"

"Today?"

"Tonight." He shrugged. "But to ensure you're not overwhelmed, your assistant, Alea, and the wedding planner will discuss your agenda, make sure you're comfortable with your various duties, as well as answer any question you might have with your schedule. I think you'll find both women most helpful."

She suppressed a wave of panic. A wedding planner. A personal assistant. How many handlers did she need? "I'm quite capable of handling the preparations myself."

"I realize you have a great deal of experience at planning receptions and the sort, but you're to be my wife, Queen of Baraka. It wouldn't do to have you inundated with fatiguing details. I've brought in the most competent professionals available. I know you'll like your staff—"

"But I don't need a staff!"

"You do." He smiled almost benevolently. "It'll help you manage the stress."

"I don't feel any stress."

He smiled even more benevolently. "You will."

Actually, she had lied. She was feeling unbelievable stress at the moment. If she couldn't get out of Baraka...if she couldn't get her sister and Lilly to the States...if the wedding went forward without an escape route...

To hide her worry, Nic opened the bound leather calendar and skimmed the pages, noting the various names and dates written in. Meet personal assistant, first Arabic lesson, first fitting for wedding gown, selection of wedding ring, second Arabic lesson, first engagement party, culture lesson, third Arabic lesson, city tour with King Nuri, fourth Arabic lesson. And on and on all the way until the wedding.

Eighteen days of activities. Eighteen endless days of pretending to be somebody she wasn't. Eighteen days of acting as if she were about to become King Nuri's queen. "I have something scheduled every day."

"Exactly."

It boggled her mind. He'd thought it all out. He was *training* her for the wedding. Language lessons, beauty lessons, public appearances, private activities with her betrothed. It was a whirlwind of activity to ensure a smooth wedding and transition into married life. "King Nuri—"

"Malik," he gently corrected.

"Malik," she amended, wondering where to even start with her concerns. "Is this all necessary?"

"You're to be Queen."

"Yes, but some of this can happen after the wedding. The language lessons...the cooking classes..."

"It is better to take care of as much as possible now, before the wedding." His tone allowed for no argument. "I expect you'll be carrying my child soon after the wedding, and I understand some women do not feel up to much activity in their first trimester. My desire is to simplify your life so that after the wedding you are free to concentrate on the family."

This was definitely not part of the plan.

The plan was to rescue Lilly via America—*not* get stuck here in Baraka with a wedding ring on her finger and a sultan's baby in her womb. "You want to try for children immediately?" Nic prayed she didn't sound as horrified as she felt. Nic loved kids—other people's kids. She wasn't the nesting sort. Felt no intense maternal urges. Had never been one to want to hold the babies when friends came by the palace with their latest.

"But surely you want more children?"

More, that's right. He saw her as a mother already. She had one daughter, what was oh, five or six or seven more?

"Yes, of course, but we're still strangers...."

"We won't be in a few weeks time." He gestured to the calendar she held limply in her hand. "If you'll check your schedule you'll see we spend a significant amount of time together every day. Some days we'll be dining alone. Some days we'll be entertained. Other days we'll be shopping for necessities like a marriage bed."

Marriage bed. A fate worse than death.

Nic felt the blood drain from her face. She didn't want a marriage bed. She wasn't going to share any bed with Malik Roman Nuri, especially no bed that had "husband and wife" hung over it.

Making love was one thing. Getting married for the rest of your life was another. Unfortunately, King Nuri had them on a fast track to the ceremony, and right now, he was providing no loopholes.

Wasn't this just what Grandfather Remi had predicted? He'd said for years that one day Nic was going to meet the man who was more than her match.

"Not all men are going to roll over and play dead just because you snap your fingers," Grandfather had said. "There are men who can be shaped, directed, and then there are men who do the shaping."

Malik watched her face, seeing the wariness in the princess' blue eyes. He'd never seen a less eager bride in his life. But then, he understood some of her apprehensions. When he realized he'd have to marry, he'd had plenty of his own.

He was marrying out of necessity. The issue of succession had become more pressing since the assassination attempt last year. His younger brother, Kalen, wasn't about to leave London, having renounced all ties to Baraka and his royal family. Malik had sisters with young sons, as well as numerous male cousins, but none had remained in Baraka, all choosing Western culture over their own.

That left the issue of succession to him. He needed heirs. Boy or girl, it didn't matter. He could rewrite law, change the rules. The key was having a direct descendant. And he'd chosen the Princess Ducasse to bear him that descendant. "I don't want you to worry," he added soothingly. "I shall be a loyal, monogamous husband dedicated to fulfilling my responsibility as husband and mate."

Nic's head spun, the words husband and mate swimming through her tortured brain. *Mate…mate…mate.* "Most royals have separate bed chambers," she said at length, fingers knotting around the calendar. "Is that not the custom here?"

"My parents always shared their bed."

"Ah."

"Yours did not?" he swiftly rebutted.

She was losing focus. King Nuri was too smart, too fast, too sharp. He was taking their discussion places she really didn't want to go. "My parents had a love marriage." Her parents' marriage had been scandalous. Surely he would have heard of it even here.

Her parents had married against the wishes of her father's parents and it'd been shocking at the time, the golden boy, Prince Julien marrying the trashy American pop star. Everyone said the marriage wouldn't last the year. It lasted ten, and they were still together, still happy together when they died in the car accident on the coastal road near St. Tropez.

Nic glanced at the calendar in her hand, the edge of the small appointment book pressed to her palm. "Apparently I meet my staff in an hour and a half."

"After you freshen up. Tea and sandwiches will be served to you in your room. You'll even have time for a short nap."

Suddenly her temper snapped and she turned the little leather book around, flashing the pages. "Really? Are you certain? I don't see it in my calendar."

King Nuri didn't even glance down at the book. He simply stood there, considering her. After a moment he said, "If you do not want this marriage, Princess Chantal, say so."

The quiet authority in his voice echoed in the elegant salon. Ashamed that she'd so completely blown her cool, Nic slowly closed the leather book, drawing it against her chest. "I'm sorry."

He waited until she looked up from the intricate pattern of the crimson carpet at their feet. "I do not hold a gun to your head, Princess. This isn't obligatory. If you are dissatisfied with me as a groom, speak now. This is the time to break off the plans, not one week before the ceremony, not one day before the ceremony. The wedding is a fortnight away. We have not yet publicly celebrated. If you have reservations, tell me. I will not judge you, and I promise I will not be angry or cruel."

His words streamed in and out her ears, but the only thing she heard was the phrase, *if you have reservations*...

She *only* had reservations. Nothing about this was right. Nothing they were discussing was going to come to pass. She was a hypocrite. She was standing here, lying to him, intentionally deceiving him.

But how could she tell him the truth? If she told him who she really was, and why she was in Baraka, the engagement would be off, his assistance would end, and all efforts to free Lilly and Chantal would be for naught. No, she couldn't tell him. Couldn't stop what she'd started until they were in America, Chantal and Lilly secreted away and Nic was boarding the first plane home.

"Well?" he quietly prompted, clearly at the end of his patience.

He'd never forgive her for dumping him at the last minute. He'd never ever forgive her family for humiliating him...

Nic closed her eyes, forced herself to block out everything but little Lilly's delicate face. Lilly, like a butterfly, so small, so fragile, so painfully vulnerable.

Just thinking of Lilly trapped in La Croix made Nic's temper flare. How could people...society...be so unjust? Girls should be raised without fear and intimidation. Girls should be protected.

She opened her eyes, met Malik's dark gaze. "My only reservation is that I am to be married so far from those I love." *Lie, lie, lie.* She wanted to be married in America only because the country was vast, Louisiana was clannish, and her mother's network of old friends and distant relatives would definitely provide cover for Chantal and Lilly once they went into hiding. "I would feel much more comfortable if you'd be willing to consider my…thoughts…my request.''

He stared at her for a long, heated moment, before inclining his head. ''If it means so much to you, yes. I shall consider your thoughts, and think more on your request.''

Nicolette felt a dizzying wave of relief. She could do this, she told herself, encouraged. She'd pull this off yet. ''Thank you, Your Highness.''

''But of course. I want you happy. Our wedding is special. The day of the wedding will be a national holiday in Baraka. The ceremony shall be televised, so all our people can celebrate with us.''

No pressure there. ''Excellent.'' Some of her relief faded. Standing up the sultan in front of hundreds of thousands of his people was not her idea of a good time. ''What a fabulous idea.''

''Thank you.'' His silver gaze glinted. ''Now let me show you to your suite. I'm sure you could use some time alone.''

In her room, Nicolette fished out her own pocket organizer from the bottom of her suitcase and flipped quickly through her scribbled notes. Hotels, rental cars, bank numbers, phone numbers, maps of downtown Baton Rouge and vicinity. She'd already wired money to the Bank of Louisiana's Baton Rouge branch, bought a used car, had it gassed and prepped with maps and an emergency road kit, and spoken to the priest at her mother's childhood church. Everything was set. Everything would work. It was simply a matter of getting them there.

It seemed as though no time at all had passed before a knock on her door forced Nic to zip her notes back into the inner compartment of her suitcase. She ran her fingers through her hair and opening her door, discovered a cluster of women in the hall. Nicolette's new staff had arrived.

For two hours the women chatted, introducing themselves, explaining how each would assist the princess. They all spoke excellent English.

The wedding planner was young and very efficient but there was little opportunity to discuss the wedding in detail. Nicolette's assistant, Alea, was beautiful with dark hair and kind eyes and there were numerous other maids as well who fussed over the princess. Nicolette's head spun with all the names and various duties. She'd never had this much help in her life.

At nine fifteen, Nic's bedroom door opened again, and an attractive young woman, elegantly dressed in a vivid emerald-green gown with elaborate gold embroidery at the seams, entered Nic's room.

The other women sitting with Nic immediately rose and bowed. "Welcome, my lady," they all chorused, several falling into deep curtsies.

The young woman—close to Nicolette's own age—approached Nic with a cool smile. "I'm sorry I'm late." She stopped before Nic, and she took a moment to scrutinize Nicolette from head to toe. "I am Lady Fatima, cousin to the sultan, a member of the royal family. I've been asked by my cousin to help you adjust to our customs."

Fatima's words were polite but Nic heard the aloof note in Lady Fatima's voice. Lady Fatima did not intend for them to be friends. But Lady Fatima didn't need to feel threatened. Nic had no intention of permanently staying. The sooner she and the Sultan headed to America, the sooner the charade could end.

The women finally left close to midnight, and Nic fell into bed exhausted.

There were too many people getting involved, she thought, curling on her side, too many people spelled trouble.

But you're already in trouble, a little voice mocked her, and she bunched her hand in her silk coverlet, knowing that if she wasn't very careful, she could soon be trapped in Atiq forever, married to the sultan, mother to his sons. And Grandfather Remi would have the last laugh of all.

Nic, married.

Nic, Queen of Baraka. Royal Babymaker.

Nic didn't usually wake up in a bad mood, but her dreams had been so intense, so upsetting, that by the time she headed into her mammoth adjoining bathroom with the enormous white and sunken tiled tub, dread filled every muscle and pore.

She needed to talk to Chantal. She needed advice quickly. There'd never been a back up plan, and that was a mistake. Nic realized now that they should have discussed emergency measures, like other destination alternatives to America, and how to extricate Nic from the engagement without creating an international scandal.

Not waiting for the bath to completely fill, Nic sat in the tepid water, soaped up with the scented bath gel and quickly rinsed off before dressing. She usually thought fast on her feet but right now she had no ideas, no answers, no possible escape routes.

The *Royal Star* had returned to Melio. She'd traveled without a great deal of cash. Even if she wanted to run, how on earth would she get out of here?

Well, if you really had to run, you could always tell him the truth, the little voice chanted as Nic combed her long dark hair, pulling it back into a smooth coil at her nape.

But if you tell him the truth, Lilly remains in La Croix.

Not if he develops feelings for you...

It's horrible to use a man like that.

Yet lots of men have developed feelings for you, and you've never worried overly much about hurting them before...

A knock sounded on her door. Relieved to escape the conflict of her conscience, Nic took the bobby pin from her mouth and tucked it into the coil of hair at her nape. "Come in."

Malik entered her room. "Am I interrupting anything?"

She pulled another pin open with her teeth and plucked it into the coiled mass. "I'm just doing my hair."

He entered her room, closed her door behind him. "You do have beautiful hair."

The sincerity of the unexpected compliment made her flush. "Thank you."

"I've always loved hair that color. I was admiring the shade yesterday."

Nic didn't know what to say. It was a bottle-brown, something Nic had washed in herself. "I'm flattered, Your Highness."

"It's odd," he continued, "but I've never been attracted to blondes."

Nic's hand shook, and the coiled hair, not properly anchored, slipped loose, delicate pins tumbling free. "You don't like blondes?" Men *loved* blondes.

"Not particularly."

"Why not?"

"I don't want to be stereotypical, but..."

"But what?"

"Well, in my experience, I've found most blondes to be...shallow. Self-absorbed. Less intellectual."

Nic blinked to chase away the veil of red before her eyes. *In his experience.* What kind of blondes had he met? "My sister, Nicolette, she's a natural blonde, and she's extremely intelligent."

"Really?" He frowned skeptically.

"Yes," Nic answered firmly, outraged that he could hold such a ridiculous prejudice against women based on hair color. "Nic holds advanced degrees in mathematics and science."

"Speaking of your sister," he said, changing topics. "That's why I've come. As we're not married yet, I wouldn't normally visit your room uninvited, but since your sister called, I thought it might be urgent."

"Which sister?"

"I could have sworn she said Chantal."

"Impossible." Chantal must have made a mistake and said her own name.

"Exactly." His gaze met hers and held. "Chantal's here."

"Maybe it was Joelle. Sounds a bit like Chantal."

"Maybe."

"Or Nic," she added, seeing a spark of a smile in his eyes, and the cool mocking smile put her teeth on edge. What was he thinking? What did he know?

"Didn't sound like Nicolette," he answered, reaching into his pocket, pulling out the phone. "This sister sounded sophisticated. Refined. And from what I've heard, that's not your sister Nic."

She tensed at his criticism. He didn't even know Nicolette and yet he sounded as if he were the font of all wisdom. But he was holding the phone out to her, asking her if she wanted to take it. "Do you want to call?" he was asking. "I have the number saved."

So who would have called, Nic wondered? Her grandparents didn't even know she was here—so obviously they hadn't phoned. Joelle knew Nic was gone, but believed she'd headed off for a visit with Chantal in La Croix, leaving only Chantal to phone, but that wasn't a call Nic wanted to make in front of King Nuri. "I can phone later."

His expression didn't change. His arm remained extended,

offering the slim phone. He was dressed casually today, khakis, crisp white shirt, the sleeves rolled up a couple times on his forearms. "It could be urgent. Just hit Redial."

Nic tried not to glare at him as she took the phone, moving past him to stand at the window overlooking a pretty interior courtyard. Pressing the redial button, Nic heard the phone ring and almost immediately was connected with Chantal.

"Thank goodness it's you," Chantal said, wasting no time on preliminary greetings. "I've been worried sick."

"No reason to worry. Everything's fine." *Lie again.*

"So how is it going?"

Nic knew she couldn't tell Chantal the truth. Chantal was the typical first born, big sister. A worrier, overly responsible, Chantal was also a guilt-ridden perfectionist. The last thing she needed was one more reason to blame herself. "I'm fine. Honestly."

Chantal hesitated. "How…how is he?"

Nic tried to close her eyes and blot out King Nuri's presence, but he wasn't easy to dismiss, and even with her back turned, Nicolette felt his proximity. The man radiated energy. "Okay."

"Is he giving you any trouble?"

"No." Nic glanced over her shoulder, caught Malik's eyes. He'd been watching her with interest. As well as amusement. "How is Lilly?"

Chantal let out a small breath. "We're making plans. I've been in contact with mother's high school friend, Andrea. She's agreed to help us once we reach Baton Rouge."

"Good."

There was a moment of silence on the line. "I appreciate what you're doing," Chantal said quietly. "I'm not sure it's the right thing—I still think it's awfully risky for you—"

"No regrets," Nic interrupted. "No second thoughts, either. This is for Lilly. I love her dearly. You know that."

"I do."

"Okay." Nic's heart felt tight. There was so much at stake. Just hearing her sister's voice made Nic realize all over again how much depended on her. "We'll talk soon."

The call ended, Nic returned the phone to King Nuri. "Thank you. You're right. The call was important."

"I heard you mention your daughter. I trust she's fine?"

Nic saw Lilly's wide blue eyes, already too troubled. Four-year-old children weren't supposed to worry so much. "Yes."

"When is she going to join you?"

"Soon." Nic mustered a tight smile. "I hope."

He nodded, hesitated. "I don't see you again until later this evening, and I imagine you've looked over today's agenda. Did you have any questions?"

His question suddenly reminded her of why she'd woken in such a lousy mood. He might exude raw sensuality, but he was nothing short of a dictator. "I'm not a child, Your Highness."

"I didn't think you were."

She felt her temper swell, her anger was fueled by completely contradictory emotions. She'd never been so attracted to anyone before, and yet he was entirely unsuitable for a relationship. "So why have you—without consulting me, or asking for any input—put me back into school? According to my schedule, I have classes from morning until afternoon, starting with a two-hour Arabic lesson in fifteen minutes."

"I've done only what is necessary—"

"Forgive me, Your Highness," she interrupted sharply, "but these are decisions I should be making for myself. Perhaps here men decide for the women, but in my country women have a say about what happens in their lives."

CHAPTER THREE

His cool silver gaze rested on her face, his eyes touching her lips, her nose, her cheeks, her eyes. "A man naturally wants what is best for his woman."

She felt a shiver race down her spine. His woman. But she wasn't his woman. She had no intention of ever becoming his woman. "A woman finds it difficult to respect a man that doesn't allow her to use her brain."

"This isn't a political exercise, Princess Thibaudet. I'm simply asking you to study our language and culture—"

"All day long."

His jaw tightened. "It's not as if you're actually in school. You'll be studying with my cousin Fatima, who is not only a member of the royal family, and close to your age, but a true Barakan scholar. I expect that the two of you will become great, close friends."

Great, close friends? Nic flashed back to last night, and Fatima's cool welcome. The Sultan was dreaming. "Yes, I've met Lady Fatima, and Your Highness, my frustration isn't with the teacher, but the lessons themselves. I'm concerned that less than twenty-four hours after arriving I've already lost—" she broke off, biting back the word *control*.

She wasn't upset because she was going to learn a new language. She was upset because she was quickly losing control...of the wedding, her environment, her independence itself. Nic had spent her entire life fighting to keep the upper hand and yet less than twenty-four hours after arriving she felt as if she'd become a possession instead of a woman.

Nic struggled to find a more diplomatic way to say what she was feeling. "I'm asking you, Your Highness, to give me more input into organizing my schedule. I'd find the lessons and activities less objectionable if I had a choice."

35

"But what would you do differently? Everything I've chosen for you is good for you."

He didn't get it. Because he was a man, and a powerful man, he didn't understand what it was like to be told where to go, when to go, how to get there. "But that's precisely my point, Your Highness. Women want to choose for themselves!"

He sighed, glanced at his watch, and shook his head. "As interesting as this is, I've people waiting in my office, and I'm afraid I've spent all the time on this discussion that I intend to spend. I regret that you're unhappy with my choices, but I expect you'll enjoy the lessons once begun."

And that was it. He was done. He turned away, headed for the door and Nic watched his departing back in astonishment. He was serious. He was really done.

The fact that he'd walk out on her blew her mind. Her temper surged yet again. "I'm not going to the lessons," she called out. "I'll look my schedule over and see if I can't adapt the activities to better suit my needs."

Ah, that caught his attention. She suppressed a smile of satisfaction as he stopped at the door, and slowly turned around. His silver gaze grew flinty, his expression implacable. "The lessons are set."

"Nothing in life is set." She lifted her chin, temper blazing, emotions high. "And I won't be dictated to. If you wish a marriage with a modern princess, than you'd better expect a modern partnership. I didn't travel this far to become a royal doormat."

His dark head cocked, his jaw rigid. "A doormat?" he repeated softly. "I find the description highly offensive. I have nothing but the utmost respect for women, and the women in my life are cherished and protected. And if you learning our language is so objectionable—"

"It's not the language, Your Highness!" She was walking toward him, frustration and irritation coiled so tightly inside her she couldn't keep still. "I've never minded learning your language, but I shouldn't have to be immediately immersed in language coursework first thing on arrival. Your country is bilingual. Everyone in Baraka speaks French. And my country is also bilingual. We speak Spanish and French."

He folded his arms across his chest. "But French is part of our colonial past while Arabic is the future."

She stopped in front of the sultan, arms folded just like him, mimicking his pose. "So why marry a European princess, Your Highness? There must be plenty of Arabic princesses if that is indeed, *your* future."

He didn't answer her question but leaned toward her, brow furrowed, and she instinctively held her breath as his lips grazed her ear. "It's not too late to put you on a plane and send you home."

She gritted her teeth, eyes narrowing. How typical. Met with conflict, he'd rather send her home than compromise. "Maybe you should. You're not ready for the reality of marriage, Your Highness."

Suddenly his hand was against the back of her neck, his fingers curled against her warm sensitive skin. She shivered. He felt the shiver and his fingers tightened perceptibly. "You can not blame me entirely, Princess. You've changed. A month ago you were most eager for this union. Two weeks ago you expressed nothing but eagerness, willingness."

He'd drawn her close, so close that she was nearly held against his chest. She could feel his body's warmth, his leashed energy, his innate strength. There was no escaping him this time. Not until he chose to let her go. "What has caused this change of heart, Chantal? You're nothing but difficult today."

"I'm not difficult. I'm merely honest." He was manhandling her, dominating her, and his arrogance infuriated her. There was no reason to trap her like this against him, render her helpless with his body...his will. "Yet it appears I'm not allowed to have an opinion."

His fingers stroked the side of her neck, his thumb drawing small circles which she found maddening. She liked his touch. She hated his dominant strength. It was as if her body loved the pleasure, but her mind detested his control.

"Of course you're allowed to have an opinion," he answered calmly. "But your opinions so far express only displeasure and discontent—"

"You can't say that based on the ninety minutes we've spent together!"

He forced her head back, ensuring that she saw his full displeasure. His jaw flexed. His silver gaze shone brittle. He was barely hanging onto his temper. "Do you ever stop and think before you speak, Princess?"

"And do you bully everyone into doing what you want, King Nuri? I understand you're the sultan, but surely, others—your family, your subjects—are allowed a modicum of free speech?"

"You've tasted more than free speech," he retorted, pressing a finger against her lips. "In fact, I've heard all I want to hear from you."

"Well, I won't be quiet!" she talked despite the finger shushing her, talked to push him away, talked to keep from falling apart. The tension between them was overwhelming and Nicolette had never been so afraid. He excited her. He terrified her. She could only imagine how wild, how explosive their love-making would be.

"You won't?"

She swallowed convulsively, feeling prickly with heat, her nerves screaming in anticipation. The tension crackling between them was unlike anything she'd ever known before. But then, she'd never challenged a man as powerful as Malik Nuri before. "No." She drew a quick, shallow breath, trying somehow to regain her footing again. She could hear Chantal in her head, hearing Chantal's disapproval. Chantal would never, ever challenge a man like this. Chantal believed in tact, diplomacy, quiet strength.

Nic's strength wasn't even close to being quiet.

But she wasn't here as Nicolette, rebel middle daughter. She was here as Chantal, and King Nuri had expected agreeable Chantal.

His head lowered, his lips brushed her cheek. "I can not have a disobedient wife."

His deep cultured voice penetrated through her, electrified the most inner part of her. Her belly clenched in a knot of pleasure and fear. She craved, physically craved, his voice, his strength, his power. She wanted him to touch her. She wanted his hands all over her.

You're mad, she choked inwardly. You've lost your mind if you want to take King Nuri on this way.

But she did. She wanted to provoke him. Test him. See how far he'd let her go. She wondered where he'd draw the line and what he'd do to make her toe the line.

Power. Control. Submission. Domination. She was strong. Very strong. So strong that she'd never met a man who could match her strength—until today. "A husband shouldn't require obedience. He should desire a spirit of cooperation, and mutual respect."

His lips hovered above her cheek. "But a woman can't respect a man if he lets her walk all over him."

"I don't believe you've allowed me to walk anywhere near you, Your Highness."

He tipped her chin up and his silver gaze burned into her eyes, seeing the fire and rebellion she couldn't possibly hide. "You refuse to capitulate."

His touch was making her head spin. "But why should I have to capitulate? If you're serious about wanting a wife with an education and a sense of self-worth, then you'd welcome my thoughts."

"I do welcome them. I just don't expect my bride to challenge every request I make."

"I'm not your bride yet, and you're not making requests. You're making demands. There's a difference. We both know it." She jerked her head back, put her hands to his chest and gave a firm push. There was no way she'd let him knuckle her under.

His gaze swept down, from her warm cheeks, to her lips and even lower to the full swell of her breasts. "And if I ask you to attend language classes?"

The weight of his gaze on her breasts made them ache. It was as if he was touching her, caressing her, and her nipples peaked, hardening. "I'd consider your request." Her voice had dropped, grown husky. He had to know what he was doing to her, had to know the sensations he was stirring within her.

His gaze slowly lifted again, traveling up her neck, over her full, soft mouth, past her flushed cheeks to her eyes. "Not everything between us needs to be a fight."

His inflection was nearly as husky as her own. She felt warmth creep through her, a seductive wash of awareness...and desire. "I'm not fighting now."

The corner of his mouth lifted in the briefest smile. "No. But I expect this is but a momentary reprieve."

Oh, that smile of his. It was dangerous. Mysterious. It was as if he knew all sorts of things about her that she didn't even know. "You don't like to fight?"

He coughed, cleared his throat. "No." His silver gaze warmed, the gray-green depths turning rich, molten. "There are too many other things I'd rather do with women, particularly if she happens to be *my* woman."

There. His woman again. More possession. And she didn't want to be a possession.

"Now let's see how well this works," he continued softly, a husky note of compulsion in his voice. "Princess Chantal, I'm asking you to please consider attending the language and culture classes that begin in—" he glanced at his watch "—fifteen minutes. It's important to me that you familiarize yourself with our culture. Can you manage to squeeze the lessons into your busy schedule?"

He really wasn't giving her a choice, though, and she knew it. He was asking her, but he was fully expecting her to say yes. Damn him. Malik Roman Nuri was really hard to manage. "I'll check my calendar," she answered crisply. "But if my morning is open, I'll do my best to make the first lesson."

His eyes gleamed. His smile was mocking. He reached for her again, his fingers curling through her long hair. "You, Princess, have had too many Western men."

His words, his touch, his knowing smile made her tremble inwardly. The power continued to shift. The boundaries seemed practically invisible. He touched her as if she was already his. And her body was responding to him as if it were the most natural thing in the world. "I said I'd try."

He released her leisurely, drawing his fingers from her thick hair even more slowly. "You will. We both know you will. You're in Baraka now, *laeela*. My will, Princess, will soon be your command." Taking her hand in his, he kissed her knuckles. "Enjoy your time with Fatima. I'll look forward to getting a full report on your lessons tonight."

Nic watched him leave, feeling a bubble of hysteria form in her chest. How was she going to convince him to go to America? How was she going to convince him to do anything? He wanted her to submit—not the other way around!

You're in so much trouble, she told herself, feeling like a ship with a hole in the stern. She was going to sink. The only question was how much time did she have left before she went down?

Nicolette met Fatima in an airy salon, where the wood shutters at the tall arched windows were folded back, allowing the bright sun to bounce off the pale apricot walls and drench the marble floor with its dramatic black and ivory diamond pattern.

The language lesson seemed to last forever, but then a serving girl carried in almond pastries and mint tea.

Fatima poured the tea, glancing at Nicolette as she did so. "You know we have a saying here, Princess Thibaudet. *There's no escaping death and marriage.*" Fatima smiled grimly, handed Nicolette her tea cup. "It's true, you know. A girl's place is in the home. Tending to the family."

Nic shrugged, sensing the other woman's hostility thinking of the life Chantal had lived so far in La Croix, knowing that they were supposedly discussing Chantal's future, not hers. "I don't have a problem with that, Lady Fatima. I have a daughter. I'm comfortable being home. I've lived this way for years."

Fatima blew delicately on her hot tea. "Your daughter will marry a man chosen for her, too, then?"

Nic startled, picturing her young niece being forced to marry against her will. Never. "There's no reason for Lilly to do that."

"Yet…if you are to marry the Sultan," Fatima's smile was hard, and it made her dark eyes gleam like polished onyx, "your other children will have to follow our traditions. Surely it would be better for Lilly to do the same."

Nicolette couldn't answer. She felt cold on the inside. Scared, too. "Your cousin has never spoken of this to me."

"Not yet, no. But he will. After I have introduced our culture to you." Fatima sipped from her cup. "That is my job, you realize. To introduce you to our ways."

Nic stared into her small cup, her emotions growing hot, replacing the ice around her heart. Had Chantal considered this? Thank God Chantal was not here. Thank God she would not have to listen to this. Be tortured like this. Chantal and Lilly had been through too much already.

Gracefully Fatima set her cup on the low table, lifted the plate of pastries out to Nicolette. "Please."

It'd be impossible for Nic to eat now. She'd choke on the pastry. Her throat was dry as dust.

Fatima inclined her head. "Back to our discussion about your daughter. Do you really think it is fair to her to make her an outcast? To treat her differently than you'll treat your children with the sultan? Please try to think of it from her perspective, of what would benefit her most. How do you think she will feel being different? And how shall your choices impact her later? Because, Princess, no Barakan man will ever marry her, and if she can't marry here then you are choosing to send her far away."

Nic's tongue pressed to the roof of her mouth. She felt horribly close to choking. "She's *four*, Lady Fatima. Just four years old. A little girl still. I think these decisions don't need to be made for a number of years."

"Time passes quickly."

Not quickly enough, Nic silently retorted, furious, hanging on to her temper—barely. Fatima's company was becoming intolerable. "And you," Nic said, turning the focus onto the twenty-five-year old. "What are your cousin's plans for you? Is there a husband on the horizon, or are you going to remain here, devoting your life to him and me?"

Fatima's eyes narrowed. "I haven't heard who he has selected for me, but I am interested, of course. Why? Have you heard something?"

"No."

For the first time since they sat down together this morning, Fatima expressed uncertainty. "But if you do hear something, you'll tell me?"

"Of course, Lady Fatima. We should help each other, not hurt each other, don't you think?"

Returning to her room, Nic glanced at her calendar, unable to believe that every morning would be spent in virtual hell with Fatima, unnerved by the fact that she was making every decision—including decisions about meals and coffee—based on a calendar. *Malik Nuri's calendar!* It was an insult to her intelligence. A test of her control.

Insult or not, Nic knew that according to the calendar, she had just enough time to freshen up and change before dinner. According to her appointment book, she and King Nuri would be dining alone together, and Alea had clothes already waiting, a pale pink trouser set with a long slim silk overcoat.

Nicolette wasn't in the mood for pink, but she didn't have the energy to protest, especially not when she had more pressing matters on her mind.

Managing her emotions—and reactions—around the sultan was an issue. Lady Fatima was already posing a problem. And Nicolette was no closer to convincing the sultan that the wedding should be moved to Baton Rouge than when she arrived yesterday afternoon.

So think of tonight as an opportunity, she told herself, as she was escorted to King Nuri's quarters. This isn't a chance to fail, but a chance to succeed.

They ate Western style, sitting at a small table in one of the elegant courtyards. Torches illuminated the tiled walls, reflecting off the ancient mosaics decorating every surface. During the meal, Nic struggled to think of a natural way to bring up her concerns about the wedding—and Lady Fatima—but no opportunity presented itself. But the wedding first.

"I attended the lessons today," she said, cringing a little at her inept opening. There had to be a better way to approach the topic than this. "Lady Fatima is certainly…knowledgeable."

"She is, isn't she?"

Nic forced herself on. "She expressed thoughts that troubled me."

"Indeed?"

He wasn't being very helpful here. "Despite her education, she sounds quite conservative, at least in terms of women's roles in your society."

His shoulders shifted and the candle light flickered over his face, his features even, controlled. "Fatima has always been most comfortable as a woman. She embraces the unique differences between men and women."

Was he purposely taunting her? "Sounds perfect for you. I'm surprised you never considered marrying her."

His gaze clashed with hers. "Did I say that?"

"Did you propose?"

"No. I respect her immensely, but she's like a sister to me."

Finally some insights into his world. Ever since arriving in Atiq, Nicolette had floundered, struggling to get her feet on the ground. Just who was Malik Nuri? What did he want? What did he really believe? "Have you ever proposed to anyone?"

"I've waited a long time to marry." His expression revealed nothing, and his tone was deceptively mild. "I've waited a long time for you."

"Not me—"

"Yes, you, Princess."

She wasn't sure what to say next. Maybe she should just be glad he'd presented her with an opportunity to address her wedding concerns. "Have you had a chance to think about my request? It really does mean a great deal to me...marrying in my mother's parish." She tried to keep her tone casual, although beneath the table her fingers were knotting her linen napkin. There were so many undercurrents between them—personal, physical, sexual.

"Your mother, the American."

"I know you want to be married here, in Atiq, but perhaps we could find a compromise. Instead of just one ceremony, we could have two. We go to Baton Rouge for my church ceremony, and then return here for a traditional Barakan ceremony."

"Two ceremonies?"

"It's not unheard of, Your Highness—"

"Malik. Please. We're discussing our wedding."

The way he said *our wedding* made her blush and she nodded awkwardly, immediately aware of the size of him, the strength of him, as well as the sense that despite the differences between them, they'd be eventually matched in bed. "Dual ceremonies are being done more and more these days," she said, voice almost breaking. "It's one way of addressing the various aspects of culture."

He hesitated, lips pursing. "Perhaps. I've never thought of drawing this out, but that's not to say we couldn't make it happen."

Yes. Nic felt herself exhale in a deep rush. But her relief was tinged by something else...an emotion far more personal, one that had nothing to do with Chantal and Lilly and only to do with her attraction.

"We'd marry here first, then," he added, as if thinking aloud. "You're already here. The plans have been made. After the palace ceremony, we could fly to Louisiana, invite your friends and family to join us there."

His words popped whatever brief fantasy she held. She was

being ridiculous, the daydream she had been having of a lazy afternoon in bed was even more ridiculous. He was a sultan. She was a princess. She wasn't even the princess he wanted. "Your Highness—" she saw his frown, and quickly substituted his name "—Malik. I appreciate you considering my suggestion, and I'm grateful you're willing to travel to the States, but if we should do all that, I'd really like to walk down the aisle first…be a bride in white."

"A bride in white," he echoed thoughtfully.

And then remembering she was supposed to be Chantal she forced a tight smile. "I know I've done it before, but it's still…traditional."

"And you're the traditional sister, right?" He leaned away from the table and the candles, having burned low, turned the table into a shade of rose-gold. "You mentioned this morning that the Ducasses are half French?"

It was a quick switch. He was very good, she thought, rinsing off her fingers in her water bowl, wiping her hands dry. He controlled the conversation. He controlled her physical reactions. He controlled her emotions. This was certainly a first for her.

"French and Spanish," Nic answered after a moment's pause, gathering her wits about her, knowing she needed them more than ever. He let nothing slide. He remembered every word she said. "Although throughout history many Ducasse kings took English brides."

"Royal brides?"

"Only royal brides."

"So you were raised speaking…?"

"French for father, English for Mother, and our nanny was from Seville, so we spoke Spanish with her."

"Any other languages?"

Her heart was no longer racing. She felt calmer again, dignified. "I read Latin, of course, know some Greek, a fair amount of Italian and can get by with my German."

"A linguist."

She shrugged. "I'm a mathematician. They say language and math use the same parts of the brain."

"Interesting." His fingers tapped the table, his expression almost brooding. "I didn't realize both you and Nicolette studied mathematics at university. I knew she had—you'd mentioned that this morning—but didn't know you had as well."

Nic gave herself a hard mental kick. You're Chantal, act like Chantal! But it was proving harder to do than Nic ever expected. Having never wanted to be anyone but herself. "It's all the same gene pool," she said lightly. The table had been covered by an elegant purple cloth shot with gold threads so the entire table seemed to glimmer and shine in the soft candlelight.

"Speaking of the parental gene pool, I met your father once," Malik said, again changing the topic, keeping her firmly off balance. Candlelight flickered across his face, playing up the length of his imperial nose, the uncompromising line of his jaw. "Years ago, when I was still in my teens, I heard him address a group of leaders at a European economic summit. He was brilliant."

"He loved Melio." Nic pictured her country's beautiful old port, the narrow tree-lined streets, the pretty farms tucked between rocky hills. "He wanted the best for Melio, and was willing to make whatever sacrifices were necessary—"

"Except for giving up your mother," the sultan interrupted thoughtfully. "Your mother wasn't ever negotiable, was she?"

Her mother, the American pop sensation…a star who'd risen from the poorest roots imaginable. Her mother had grown up hungry. Hungry for food, warmth, love, shelter. Hungry for recognition.

Only Nic's grandparents hadn't seen it that way. They'd thought her mother was hungry for power and they'd done everything in *their* power to break up Julien and Star's marriage. They'd wanted so much more for their Prince Julien. "He would have given up the crown if he had to," she answered flatly.

"Your grandparents nearly disinherited him."

She shook her head, finding it all so ludicrous. "My grandparents underestimated my mother." Nic had never visited her mother's birthplace in Louisiana, but she knew it was considered rural. Rough. Poverty stricken, crime ridden. Definitely not roots to be proud of. "Mother may have been born poor, but she wasn't afraid of challenges." No one worked harder than her mother. She had little formal schooling, having dropped out of high school before earning her diploma, but she'd dreamed big and that counted for something.

Malik's gaze rested on Nic's flushed face. "You got along well with her?"

"Very." Nic had adored her mother. In some ways they were one and the same. Fearless. Absolutely fearless. "I'm glad she wasn't your typical princess. I'm glad she was poor, blue collar, American. She took nothing for granted. She taught us to take nothing for granted."

A maid appeared with a tray and a steaming pot of coffee and two small cups. As the maid poured the coffee Nic wondered how on earth had they gotten onto this topic in the first place. It was not her favorite topic. Nic was too much like her mother to understand those who'd criticized Star.

Malik waited for the maid to leave again. "Would you say you're the same kind of mother to Lilly? What is your relationship with your daughter like?"

And suddenly Nicolette felt wrenched all over again, remembering how everything they were saying, everything they were doing was a lie. She was supposed to be playing Chantal, instead she kept speaking from the heart, answering his questions honestly, openly.

Think like Chantal...think like Chantal. And Nic could see Chantal in her mind's eye and knew that yes, Chantal was a fantastic mother. Chantal was the ultimate mother. "I think I'm more protective than my mother," Nic said after a moment. "And Lilly, I think, is more trusting than most children, and considerably more vulnerable."

Malik sipped from his small cup. "Perhaps it's losing her father so young in life."

Nic couldn't help her jaw hardening. Armand...Armand... how she hated Prince Armand Thibaudet. "Perhaps," Nic agreed quietly, but her voice came out cold, flat. "Or perhaps it's that she's very bright for her age, quite intuitive, and she senses that things are not...as they should be."

Malik stared at her, considering her, his expression curious, almost speculative. After a minute ticked by, he shifted in his chair, leaning back to make himself more comfortable, and yet the intensity of his gaze made her burn from the inside out. "From what I understand, your first marriage wasn't a love match."

Her stomach was in knots. She could hardly concentrate. "Far from it."

"Yet you came to Baraka…?"

Because I didn't have a choice, she wanted to tell him. You were pressuring Chantal, and Chantal's had enough pressure. "I want Lilly happy," she said at last, feeling the weight of the world rest on her shoulders. Somehow, in less than forty-eight hours, he'd tied her in knots. She wasn't Nic. She wasn't Chantal. She didn't know who she was anymore. The only thing she did know was that the chemistry between her and King Nuri was wild…stunning…she'd never had this kind of response to anyone and there was no way—absolutely no way—she could let the attraction get out of hand.

CHAPTER FOUR

LATER that evening, after returning to her room, she lay in bed, staring at the wood shutters where just the faintest edge of light could be made out around the edges. She couldn't sleep.

Couldn't turn her brain off.

She was beginning to worry, really worry. First her dinner conversation with King Nuri played in her head, and then as soon as that conversation ended, she heard her last conversation with Chantal begin, the conversation they had just hours before Nic had boarded the *Royal Star* yacht.

"It's just a meet and greet, right?" Nicolette had asked, drumming her fingers on her locked steamer trunk. *"You wouldn't actually marry him. It's just a chance to say hi—bye— and know what you're not getting involved with?"*

Chantal's eyebrows lifted. *"Be careful, Nic. This isn't one of your fun-loving Greeks. This is King Nuri—"*

"A man—"

"A King."

Nic shrugged. *"So he's a royal, but so are we—and just because a man says jump, it doesn't mean we have to."*

So she didn't have to jump, but the wedding was less than two weeks away and she had no idea how she was going to make this work.

What if she couldn't get out of Baraka? What if she wasn't able to break off the engagement in time?

There was no way she'd go through with this marriage.

Not even to rescue Lilly?

The little voice in Nic's head made her sigh, close her eyes. She knew she'd marry Bluebeard if it'd save Lilly. But oh, let there be another way...

There had to be another way...

Once again Nic woke up in a bad mood. She hated lies.

Detested hypocrisy. And yet here she was, about to begin another day pretending to be someone she was not.

Alea had breakfast waiting outside in Nic's private courtyard, and after wrapping herself in one of the long silk robes from her wardrobe, Nic wandered outside, pulling her hair into a ponytail high on the top of her head.

She caught a glimpse of herself in the koi pond outside. Brown hair. Long messy ponytail. Dark circles under the eyes.

Princess heading to disaster.

Alea sat with Nic while she had her breakfast. "It's going to be a busy day," Alea said, studying Nic's calendar. "Language lesson. Culture lesson. Then a wedding gown fitting—"

"No."

Alea looked up from the appointment book. "Did you want lunch before the fitting?"

"No. No, I don't want to go to the wedding gown fitting—"

"It's only scheduled for an hour."

Nic covered her face with her hands, rubbed her forehead, hating the headache that never seemed to go away. "I just wish...I mean...why can't the fitting wait?" Nic shook her head. No use complaining. Alea hadn't made the schedule and Alea couldn't change her schedule.

But Alea frowned, feeling responsible. "Do you want me to send a message to His Highness? Would you like to speak with him?"

Nic's gaze rested on the courtyard's lacy latticework, and her view through the open bedroom door to her suite of rooms. The ceiling in her bedchamber was high, and painted gold and blue, the floor covered in graceful tile mosaics—all lovely, all intended to seduce the senses, subdue the will—but Nic didn't want to be seduced and subdued. She wasn't here to be charmed. And she wasn't about to be wooed.

"These rooms," Nic said, "they're incredibly beautiful. Are all bedrooms in the palace like this?"

"Oh, no, Princess. There are just a few of these special rooms. They are reserved for the sultan's favorites." Alea smoothed a page in the open appointment book.

The sultan's favorites? As in plural. Very nice. Nic's eyebrows lifted satirically and she glanced around once more seeing the palatial use of space, large outdoor sunken pool, koi pool, and colorful mosaics with fresh eyes. "This was part of the harem."

"For the sultan's chosen."

Ah, well, that was much better, wasn't it? Nic thought pushing away from the table, thinking it fitting that she moved from one excruciating test to another. Breakfast in the harem followed by Arabic lesson with the cousin. How could life get any better?

Nic survived the arduous lesson, and then happily the study turned to geography. Today Fatima pulled out a map of Baraka and its neighboring countries and Nicolette loved learning about the various geographical points of interest—the mountain ranges, the river, the great deserts.

Abruptly Fatima folded the map. "What do you know about our weddings?"

"Very little," Nic answered, wondering why Fatima had taken the map away. She'd been enjoying the lesson immensely and they still had plenty of time left. At least fifteen minutes.

"You should know about our weddings," Fatima continued tersely. "They are very important in our culture, and they are very expensive." Fatima's lips curled but she didn't seem to be smiling. "Wedding celebrations generally last a week. The wedding itself takes place over several days. Yours will probably be at least three days. Each day of the wedding week you'll receive more gold and jewelry from Malik. And then finally on the wedding day, you'll be carried in on a great table, covered in jewels and all the gifts Malik has given you."

Nicolette was appalled, disgusted that she'd be paraded about on a table like a roasted pig at Christmas.

"You are very lucky," Fatima added forcefully. "You are grateful for your good fortune, aren't you?"

A murmur of voices sounded from the doorway and Nic glanced over her shoulder to see the servants bowing. King Nuri had entered the room and Nic couldn't be more relieved.

"Good morning," Fatima greeted, rising.

"How is the lesson coming?" he asked, approaching them, wearing dark casual slacks and a long-sleeve shirt the color of burnished copper. The shirt flattered his complexion, enhancing his features and the inky black of his hair.

"Good," Fatima said stiffly. "We're done."

"Fine. Then allow me to steal my princess." He bent his

head, kissed Nicolette on each cheek, and waved off Fatima, indicating she was free to go and turned to Nicolette. "You're certain the lesson went smoothly?"

She glanced up into his face. His expression was guarded. She wondered if he'd heard something when he first entered the room. "It went smoothly. Your cousin is quite knowledgeable."

"She is," he agreed. "And at times a little formal." He hesitated a moment. "I thought I heard her speak of our wedding customs."

So he had heard something. "She was describing the ceremony. I must admit, it seemed a little...otherworldly to me."

"Which part?"

She felt heat rise to her cheeks and tried to shrug casually. "The part where the bride is draped in gold and jewels and carried in, reclining on a table."

He laughed, the sound deep and husky, and far too sexy. "It's not exactly the same thing as walking down an aisle in virginal white, is it?"

It amused him, this little play acting of hers. The princess was determined to stick with the role, even though it didn't suit her at all.

He'd known she was Nicolette from the moment she arrived, and yet he'd gone along with her charade, curious to see how far she'd let this go. He'd heard she was tough—spirited—independent, and her fire intrigued him. As well as challenged him. She might be a player, but so was he. He'd play her game. And he'd beat her at her own game.

Watching her face now, he secretly hoped she would give him a good run for his money. Women had always fallen at his feet, swept away by his power and money. Women had always been...too easy. But Nic wasn't easy. And he liked that.

The fact that she'd come to his country and try to play him...now that was daring. She was a born risk-taker. Good for her. Too many people played it safe throughout life.

"Should we go try on that wedding gown now?" he asked, feeling almost guilty for enjoying himself so much. And yet it'd been a long time since he'd felt so enthusiastic, or optimistic, about anything.

He saw how the word "wedding gown" made Nicolette's jaw clench. It was all he could do to keep his expression blank.

"You're going to accompany me to the fitting?"

"Why not?" he answered with a shrug.

The tip of her pink tongue appeared, briefly touched the edge of her teeth. "Is it customary?" But she didn't give him chance to answer as she immediately continued. "Because somehow I can't imagine it's allowed here. According to your cousin Fatima, the men and women are still so segregated. Once girls hit puberty, women begin to lead separate lives..." Her voice drifted off. She tried again. "Perhaps I've misunderstood her, or perhaps I've misunderstood you."

"No. You didn't misunderstand."

She waited for him to elaborate but he didn't. She swallowed. "But aren't you...I'd think you'd be...as sultan..." Her confusion showed in her eyes. "More traditional."

It was rather refreshing to see her struggle. Very little gave Princess Nicolette pause. She'd arrived here thinking she had the upper hand. She'd do this, and do that, and it would be just as she planned.

But nothing in life went just as one planned. And the game was on.

"Alas," he sighed, "I am not the most traditional sultan. I've traveled a great deal, lived abroad. I hope you are not disappointed."

He felt her gaze as they walked through the palace, down one mysterious corridor and then another. She was thinking, and she was struggling to come up with some definitive conclusions but so far she hadn't.

She couldn't.

She didn't really know him.

He smiled on the inside. He liked her. He'd liked her for a long time, not that he knew her well, either. But he appreciated what he saw, admired her attitude. He knew she was the Ducasse princess who didn't want to marry. He'd heard all about her escapades, the problems she'd created in Melio, the headaches she'd given her beloved grandparents. He'd heard, too, how she didn't worry about what others thought—she loved her family—but she wasn't going to give up herself just to please them, either.

Like her, he'd dated extensively. He'd never worried about marriage, had known he'd have to marry one day, after all, he was the eldest son of the powerful Sultan Baraka, and he'd assumed that his bride would be loving, loyal, dutiful, and he'd imagined a quiet woman from his own country. But after the attempt on his life, his priorities changed.

He needed more than a quiet, obedient bride. He needed a woman who could face the challenges of life with courage, intelligence and humor.

They'd reached the end of the hall, and Malik opened the door to a very modern salon. The salon was outfitted with low couches covered in bright orange and violet velvet fabrics, the pale yellow walls were sheeted in long mirrors, and in the middle of the room was a small curtained platform for wardrobe fittings.

An elegant woman entered the room, and she bowed to King Nuri, and then turned to Nicolette. "Your Highness," she said, smiling. "It is an honor to meet you, and an even greater honor to dress you for your wedding. You must be quite excited."

Excited was the last word Nic would have used to describe her emotions at the moment. Dread, disgust, terror, anxiety, fear…those were the emotions she felt right now as she stepped up onto the platform.

"Do you have any thoughts on the type of gown you'd like to wear?" The designer asked, summoning two assistants who helped begin with the measurements.

Nic felt King Nuri's watchful presence, and she glanced up at the curtains hanging from the ceiling. She knew the curtains could be closed, offering greater privacy, but no one moved to shut them. "No. I don't really spend time thinking about these things."

"You'd never had any ideas about the gown? The color, the style, the fabric."

Nic shook her head. Once, four or five years ago, she and her sisters had spent the night before Chantal's wedding to Prince Armand planning their futures and Nic and Joelle had sketched their wedding dresses and described the kind of wedding they'd each have. Nic had said she'd do a Sleeping Beauty wedding, all pink and coral and green, because she'd have to be Sleeping Beauty to get married—go to sleep, wake up with a kiss and get dragged to the altar fast before she knew what was happening.

Joelle and Chantal had laughed, of course, but now the idea of being dragged to the altar fast appeared incredibly real.

With the measurements taken, the designer summoned for fabric samples, and the assistants carried out bolt after bolt, displaying them first before the sultan and then draping them across Nicolette's shoulder.

The fabrics were all costly—rich delicately woven silks with even more delicate threads of gold. The colors were exquisite, sheer pastel hues ranging from grass-green to young lemon, the pink of dawn to the coral plucked from the sea.

"This is just the beginning," the designer said. "Later many dedicated hands will embroider fantastic patterns, but first we must find the right silk for you."

Malik had been watching everything closely from his position on one pumpkin-hued sofa. He suddenly spoke to the designer in Arabic.

The designer listened attentively, bowed and turning to Nic, she smiled. "You are very fortunate, Your Highness, the sultan wishes you to have a gown made from each."

Nic wished everyone would stop telling her how fortunate she was. She did not feel fortunate. She felt trapped. And a gown of each color would only trap her more.

Turning, she glanced at King Nuri where he reclined on the plush sofa. His rust-colored shirt had fallen open at the collar, exposing the higher plane of his chest. He was all hard, honed muscle.

She tried not to imagine how lovely all that hard, honed muscle would be naked. She was already far too aware of him, far too attracted to him. The last thing she needed was proof of his sensuality…sexuality…virility. "I appreciate your generosity, Your Highness, but I do not need so many expensive gowns."

"It gives me pleasure to dress you," he answered lazily, a spark of possession in his eyes.

Nic swallowed, thinking she didn't like the possessive light in his eyes, or the expense, and waste, of gowns she'd never wear. She wouldn't be here long enough to wear even one of them. "I understand you are a generous man—"

"Proud, too."

The pitch of his voice made her stomach flip. He looked so relaxed, and yet she felt distinctly uneasy. Was she imagining the note of warning in his voice?

Shaken, Nic looked down, saw the latest bolt of fabric wrap

her breast and hips, the silk a wispy blue like the blue of the sky after a hard cleansing rain. She liked the blue. It made her feel almost calm.

"And one of the blue silk, too," he said, breaking the silence. "That is my favorite so far."

The fitting ended soon after, concluding in silence. The designer bowed deeply to the sultan, thanking him profusely, and then excused herself leaving Nic and King Nuri alone.

Nic heard the great wooden door softly close behind the seamstress. She remained where she was on the dais, feeling strangely alone, and unusually foolish.

"Which will be my wedding gown?" she asked, stepping off the platform and adjusting the band collar on her simple white linen overcoat and long slim skirt.

The sultan cocked his head. "Does it matter?"

No. It didn't matter. She'd only been making conversation, trying to fill the awkward silence. It wasn't as if she'd ever wear the gown anyway. "You're angry with me."

"No. Not at all." He extended a hand to her. "Come. Sit here with me so we might speak more comfortably."

She moved to sit on a sofa across from his but he shook his head. "Here." He placed a hand on the pumpkin silk sofa where he reclined.

Gingerly she sat next to him. "Comfortable?" he asked.

She ignored the mockery underlying the question. "Yes." Maybe he wasn't angry, but there was something on his mind.

He adjusted one of the gorgeous gold tapestry pillows, placing it behind her back. "Better?"

"I wasn't uncomfortable."

"Yes, but one could always feel more peace…more pleasure." He folded his arms behind his head, studied her face, her expression outwardly serene. "Did you enjoy the fitting?"

"I think I mentioned before that I'm not particularly fashion conscious."

"But the newspapers and magazines are always proclaiming your strong sense of fashion. Aren't you the clear favorite in the design world?"

Chantal was, of course. Every designer loved to dress the very slender, and inherently elegant, Chantal Thibaudet, the beautiful widowed princess of La Croix. Chantal had been beloved as the eldest Ducasse daughter, but once married and widowed, the public embraced her even more.

Nic's emotions ran riot. Chantal didn't obsess about fashion. She'd always been stylish, even sophisticated. The family used to joke that even as a baby Chantal would tug on her bonnet until it had a jaunty angle.

But Nic found the public's love affair with beautiful, fashionable princesses burdensome. She'd rather spend a day figuring math problems than go clothes-shopping. "One of the drawbacks of being in the public eye, is the constant pressure to maintain one's image. I've often felt there is too much value placed on appearances, Your Highness. I personally dislike having to worry about clothes and fashion when there is so much happening in the world that is of real importance."

"You always surprise me." The sultan smiled, and it was a genuine smile, one that reached his eyes and made the grooves along his mouth deepen. The warmth of the smile was almost unbearably appealing.

Nic's mouth dried. He looked so comfortable in himself, so physical and sexual at the same time. "That's good?"

"Yes." His smile faded but the warmth remained in his eyes. He exuded intelligence, as well as compassion. He wore his mantle of authority well. "Do you know why I selected you, Princess?"

It was hard to concentrate with him looking at her like that. She wanted to focus and yet she felt so many emotions that she had no business feeling. "I know you wanted better Mediterranean port access."

"But there are numerous Mediterranean ports, and numerous single European princesses interested in marriage." He hesitated, speaking each word with care. "I chose you, because I respect you. I believe you are like me. You understand the responsibilities of being a princess of the royal Ducasse family, and your loyalty, along with your sense of duty, make you an ideal mate."

Nic couldn't breathe. She felt the air settle in her chest. He had it all wrong. She lacked Chantal's sense of duty. Her loyalty was to her own family. That's why she was here. Not for Melio, but for Chantal and Lilly. "You don't worry I'd run away...fail to fulfill my obligations here?"

"You didn't in La Croix."

No, Chantal hadn't run away. Not in La Croix, not in Melio, not ever. But that's because good Chantal, first born Chantal, had been a pleaser since birth. All she'd ever wanted to do the "right" thing, and yet the thing that had driven Nic crazy was the thought, how did Chantal even know what was *right?*

Nic had never known what was *right*. She'd had to search for meaning, ask questions, test, push at each and every limitation. In her world, there'd been no "right," there had only been truth, and truth wasn't something one accepted blindly.

Truth required testing. Truth required proof.

"Marriages that are not love matches can work. They do work." His voice was deep, his tone thoughtful. "My parents had an arranged marriage which lasted fifty-some years."

"They are the lucky ones."

"Your grandparents' marriage was arranged. They are still together today, and you can not tell me they do not care deeply for each other."

Grandfather Remi cherished Grandmama Astrid. They were a true couple. They'd been together so long now, functioned so well together, it was as if they couldn't exist without the other. Ever since Grandmama had had her stroke, Grandfather's health had declined. Until Grandmama's stroke, Grandfather had been robust. Vigorous. Not anymore.

"They do love each other," Nic said, finding her voice. "They're wonderful people, too."

She swallowed, reminding herself that she couldn't answer just as Nicolette. She had to be Chantal. She had to think like Chantal. "Which is why I accepted Prince Armand's proposal," she added huskily. "If my grandparents thought Armand and I would be a good match, then…"

She shrugged, but she didn't feel indifferent. Armand was the lowest sort of a man, the kind that would abuse a woman verbally, physically, a man who didn't feel strong unless he completely dominated—subjugated—the woman who loved him, depended on him.

"You implied last night that Lilly wasn't happy," Malik said. "Tell me about her life in La Croix."

Nic hesitated, uncertain yet again how much she could, or should say. "It's not a positive place to raise a child."

"Yet her grandparents are there, and from what I've heard, her father's family apparently dotes on her."

"Her father's family is obsessively controlling."

"Obsessively?"

"Complete control freaks," Nic retorted, unable to hide her bitterness.

His eyebrows flattened. "An awfully American expression," he said thoughtfully. "Not one I would have ever thought you'd use. Your sister, Nicolette, now she'd say something like that…"

Could he be anymore condescending? Suddenly Nic was fighting mad. She'd love a good fight, would welcome an opportunity to spar. It was so unfair that women were trapped in bad marriages, unable to take action because mothers with young children couldn't afford to work, pay for food and shelter along with childcare. The economics alone kept women down. "Yes, she would, and she does," Nic answered hotly. "Unfortunately I've picked up some of Nic's expressions. We've just spent a week together in Melio."

"Ah." Malik's eyes narrowed slightly at the corners. "That explains it." He paused. "Because I've wondered. You haven't seemed quite yourself since you arrived. I'd always heard you, Chantal, described as gentle, controlled, emotionally contained."

"And I'm not?"

His mouth pursed. "No."

"But…but why? I think I'm exactly the same."

He shook his head. "Even your mannerisms are different. You move your body more. Your gestures are sharper, less… refined."

Ouch. Chantal the Persian cat, Nic the tiger, Joelle the lovable tabby.

"Perhaps the years at La Croix changed you." His gaze met hers, held. "Made you stronger. Fiercer. Angrier."

"Angrier?"

"You are angry."

No use even debating that one. She was angry. Deeply angry that Chantal would suffer such horrible treatment by the Thibaudets, angry that Chantal and Lilly were trapped, angry that there was no one who could help rescue them, angry that the world didn't seem to care very much when women were hurt, when women were verbally, emotionally, mentally abused.

Abuse should never be tolerated. Ever. Ever.

Children shouldn't be hurt. Women shouldn't be squashed, smashed, pushed around. Just because women were smaller boned than men, lighter in weight, softer skinned didn't mean that it was okay to make them stepping stones or punching bags.

Someone had to do something.

Someone had to care enough to say, enough is enough. I've had enough. No more.

"You're right. I am upset," Nic said after a long moment. "Very upset." She bit her bottom lip, felt the softness of the skin in her mouth and regretted that she hadn't been there for Chantal when Armand had bullied her, intimidated her. Nic was heartsick that she hadn't known Chantal's misery until too late, until the emotional scars were hidden but not at all forgotten.

She drew a slow breath to calm herself, trying to buy herself time. "I think it's easy for people to ignore those in need. I think it's easy for people to close their door, shutter their window, pretend that it's enough to take care of yourself, enough to have a full stomach and comfortable bed."

Malik's gaze grew intense. "What happened in La Croix?"

She pictured Chantal's gaunt frame, sad eyes, the abuse Nic only recently knew Chantal had suffered. "What didn't happen?"

CHAPTER FIVE

"I TAKE it your husband wasn't exactly...a good husband?" Malik's deep voice echoed concern.

Nic pressed her nails into her palm. Surely it was okay to tell the sultan this. After all, if she wanted him to help rescue Lilly, she needed his sympathy, and the only way he'd sympathize with Lilly's plight was if he knew the truth. But the truth was hard to say, painful and shameful, and Nic knew Chantal would be furious with her for speaking it aloud.

Like many abused women, part of Chantal believed that somehow she had brought the pain on herself, that she must have done something wrong along the way, that Armand's cruelty wouldn't have happened if Chantal had been a better wife, woman, mother.

Malik's long tanned fingers tapped the rim of his glass. "Did he hit you?"

Nic held her breath. The air felt hot and sharp inside her lungs. She could hear Chantal in her head, no no no, could see her sister's beautiful eyes pleading, don't say a thing, don't tell him what horrible things I went through. He'll think less of me, he'll think I'm bad, that I'm somehow...dirty.

Nic's eyes filled with tears. Damn Armand to hell. He had no right laying a hand on Chantal. No right putting his fist to her face. "Yes."

Malik's eyes searched Nic's. "Did he ever touch your daughter?"

"He was rough." Nic swallowed. She didn't like talking about her sister's marriage, didn't like airing such horrid secrets. It was shameful, she thought, understanding for the first time why Chantal couldn't talk about the abuse, why Chantal only wanted to move on. Forget.

"Were Armand's parents aware of the problem?"

Her shoulders shifted. "They couldn't have been oblivious. Armand lost his temper in front of them frequently."

"But they did nothing?"

"No. But his mother did come to me once. She'd intimated that early in her marriage Armand's father had behaved the same, but that it was our duty to forgive them, that they are good men. They just don't manage their anger well."

"She wanted you to put up with it since she had to."

Nic nodded. She'd told Chantal the very same thing. "They say abuse often perpetuates itself." She felt a gnawing restlessness. She needed to get up, move, escape this dreadful dark emotion filling her. Chantal had been through enough. Chantal would be saved. Chantal would have a chance at freedom. Independence. There was no reason for Chantal to ever have to agree to a loveless, arranged marriage again.

"I want Lilly out." Nic swallowed, forced herself to focus. "I want her away from La Croix." She drew a slow breath. "You're the only one who could possibly get her out."

"Her grandparents won't let her leave the country?"

Nic's gaze was direct. "They can be persuaded."

Malik said nothing.

Nic felt the lump in her throat grow but it only made her more determined. Lilly would get out. Chantal would be free. "There are all kinds of persuasion," she added, glancing at her hands, then up into his face. "I believe her grandparents might accept…compensation…if you will."

"Buy them off?"

"It could be possible."

"Those are desperate measures."

Nic smiled but her eyes felt hard, her skin felt cold. "And I am a desperate woman."

He stood, held out an arm. "Come, let's walk. It's feeling a little close in here."

Nic rose, slipped her trembling hands into the pockets of her slim linen overcoat, wondering if she'd alienated Malik with her honesty. Then so be it, she immediately answered. If he couldn't handle truth, if he couldn't deal with reality, then he wasn't the right one for her. Correction, the right one to help Chantal.

Because she was here for Chantal. This wasn't about her…this wasn't for her… Or was it?

Nic sucked in a breath, wondering what was happening. She was feeling a kinship with King Nuri, a new sense of belonging. But Baraka wasn't home, and wouldn't be home. Her life was in sunny Melio on the other side of the Mediterranean with its scent of cypress and oranges, shades of olive-green and dark green, the rocky cliffs and the sun drenched pastures.

Malik's arm rested lightly around her as they walked from the palace to one of the exterior courtyards, massive even by European standards, and the warmth of his body against hers flooded her with hot sensation.

She wanted so much more than just an arm on her waist. She longed to feel him all the way against her, wanted the pressure of his chest, his hips, his legs. She drew a deep breath, exhaled even more slowly. The desire to be part of him was growing stronger day by day. This was a dangerous place, she thought, and somehow the splash of fountains and the sun glinting off cobalt-blue tiles while the scent of jasmine hung in the air only added to the ache inside her.

She glanced up into his face, her gaze taking in his hard, regal features, his dark hair combed back from his broad brow. He looked pensive. Preoccupied.

"Did I shock you?" she asked, wishing she didn't care one way or the other what he thought, but she did care, she cared very much. The fact was she liked King Malik Roman Nuri more than she'd liked any man in oh—years.

He was hard, sexy, sensual. Male. She knew by the way he touched things, he understood fingers, skin, pressure, sensation. She knew by the way he moved that he was aware of himself, aware of others. Even now with his arm lightly around her waist she felt his strength and energy ripple through her, hot, sensitive, alive.

"No."

"You've gone quiet."

His palm pressed against the dip in her spine, warm, strong. Nicolette had never felt so safe. She'd never felt in danger before, but this was different. Malik Roman Nuri was a man who cared about women. Protected women. He was a man who'd always do what was right for the women in his family.

"You've given me much to think on." The pressure of his

hand eased. "I realize that you come here with unique needs of your own."

Was that a polite way of saying she had an agenda? She wasn't going to deny it. Arranged marriages were about strengthening one's position, forming an alliance, creating stability.

"We both want something," she answered frankly. "The question is, what do you *really* want from me? You already know what I want from you."

"Do I?" He shot her a curious glance. "I know you want freedom for Lilly, and stability and security for your country, but what about you? You don't strike me as a woman who has no dreams for herself."

The splash of the fountain soothed Nic's nerves. She listened to the gurgling water and it sounded cool, refreshing. She felt more at peace than she had in days. "It would be enough for me to know that my family is happy, healthy, and safe." And Nic realized that it was true. Maybe she didn't have her mother's talent and desire for fame, but she had her mother's courage. She wasn't afraid to risk all to ensure that those around her would be protected.

Nic knew she was tough. She'd always been strong. She didn't need approval. She wanted to stand on her own two feet. "And equality," she said after a moment. "Equality for women. Everywhere."

Then remembering where she was, standing in what had to be one of the most luxurious courtyards in the world, Nic realized she was speaking not just to Malik, but to a sultan, a king of a country that had once been part of the powerful Ottoman Empire, in a country where men outnumbered women in higher education ten to one.

Perhaps she'd said too much, been too honest. Nic glanced up at Malik again, tensing inwardly, waiting for his reprimand.

Instead he nodded, his expression sober. "I agree."

Another night of restless sleep. Another morning where Nicolette did not want to get up. The more Nic liked Malik, the more difficult her charade became.

But Alea wasn't about to let Nicolette spend the day in bed.

"Princess," Alea said, tugging on the covers Nicolette held over her head. "You must get up. You're going to be late."

"It's just a language lesson."

"But Lady Fatima will be waiting."

Let her wait.

"And I've Italian espresso," Alea encouraged in her cheerful singsong. "You love Italian espresso."

True, Nic loved her coffee. She could drink coffee all day. "What else do I have on my schedule?" Nic asked, her voice muffled from beneath the covers.

Alea hesitated. Nicolette knew what that meant, too. It meant that Nic had another exhausting day, lessons, appointments, luncheons—all accompanied by Fatima.

"You have the state dinner tonight, and the King will be taking you, of course." Alea was trying her best to be encouraging. "And the first of your new gowns are ready. You'll be able to wear the dress tonight when King Nuri introduces you to his aides and advisors."

Nicolette slowly lowered the covers. As much as she wanted to stay in bed and avoid the lessons and day's appointments, she knew she couldn't. She also wanted to see Malik later. Seeing him had somehow become the highlight of her day.

Several hours later, after the language lesson ended, Fatima took Nicolette on a tour of the palace, pointing out unusual details like pre-Roman bronzes unearthed at various sites in Baraka, a beautiful bronze of a young boy dating back to the start of the imperial era, gold coins that had been minted during the Almohad dynasty when Baraka was part of the territory that included Morocco, Libya, Tunisia, Algeria and part of Spain.

For a little while Nicolette forgot the tension existing between her and Fatima. Nic enjoyed the tour, finding the description of ancient treasures and artifacts riveting. She'd always loved history, was passionate about early civilizations and had once fancied herself becoming an explorer.

But in the end, after university ended, she'd never used her degrees—mathematics, history or otherwise. Instead she'd become a professional princess. For whatever that was worth.

At one point during the tour, Fatima opened a set of pale gold wood shutters, and the sun poured in. Looking out, Nicolette saw the cloudless blue sky, the far away peaks of the Atlas mountains and the not so distant date and palm trees. For a moment Nicolette felt swept back in time, sucked back one hundred, three hundred, a thousand years. Here, nothing would change quickly. Here, certain elements were constant—the burnished sun, the torrid desert, the tribal conflicts, the unwavering faith of the people.

King Malik Roman Nuri was part of these elements. He might have French ancestry, a Western education, but he was as steady and deep as the sky over the Sahara.

Maybe Chantal would like it here. Maybe Chantal would be drawn to Malik just as she, Nic, was drawn to the sultan.

Maybe she'd made a mistake telling Chantal not to come, that it'd be disastrous to accept the King's marriage proposal, because truthfully, there was great beauty here. Even the ordinary felt exotic, luxurious, mysterious. Time moved more slowly. No one was hurried, no one moved too quickly, spoke too quickly, no one seemed too busy to converse or smile—well, except for Fatima, that is.

Standing at the window, Nic tried to imagine Chantal and Lilly in Atiq, and somehow the exotic beauty overshadowed the two of them.

In her heart of hearts, Nic knew that Chantal would disappear here. Chantal would say all the proper things and agree and try to be pleasing, proper, the wife of a king, but trying hard to please another would just diminish Chantal further.

Chantal needed a life away from nobility. Service. Duty. Chantal needed to learn how to be selfish.

Nic's thoughts haunted her as they finished the tour of the palace rooms. They'd virtually viewed the entire elaborate sprawl of villas, suites and chambers. There were buildings for everything, rooms reserved for the royal family and then the formal rooms for entertaining and even the old wings were spacious, coolly elegant, steeped with a gracious mystique.

Heading back to Nic's suite in the palace, they crossed paths with Malik walking with two of his advisors.

Malik greeted her formally, using the polite Arabic greeting, kissed her on each cheek and then briefly introduced his aides.

Nicolette responded politely, murmuring words of greeting, although she couldn't remember exactly what she'd said surprised by the flood of warmth coursing through her.

She didn't know why the fleeting touch of his mouth to her skin should make her lose track of her thoughts, and yet suddenly she wasn't sure what she was doing here, or why they were all together. Uneasily she glanced up into Malik's face, and his expression was the same as it'd been when he'd briefly kissed her—cordial, considerate, attentive.

And something more.

Possession?

Nic gave herself a quick mental shake. Not possession. He didn't own her. She didn't belong here. She wasn't going to stay. Yet thinking of leaving, and leaving him, made her ache more than a little. He was tapping some emotion she usually kept buried deep inside, and this emotion had nothing to do with sex, and everything to do with life. And possibly love.

He was speaking to her now, asking a question. "How has your day been?"

"Good. Thank you." Nic struggled to find adequate words. "I'm overwhelmed by the history here, as well as the beauty. The palace is truly exquisite."

He smiled at her, creases fanning from his eyes. "I'm glad you're enjoying yourself."

She liked the way he smiled at her. It was a small smile, barely discernible, but she recognized it and knew it was for her.

Possession.

The word whispered through her head, nudging her, worrying her, reminding her of what was at stake.

But even as the warning voice whispered in her head, something peculiar was happening in her heart. She didn't feel like Chantal, the betrothed. She felt like Nicolette, the betrothed. She actually felt possessive of Malik.

But that couldn't be. She wasn't here for a relationship. She couldn't form any bonds, no attachments whatsoever. If she wanted to fall in love, let her fall in love with the country, the history, the culture.

She forced a light note into her voice. "I hope I'll have a chance to see more of the palace at a later date. It's truly wonderful. Everything has been designed with perfection in mind."

"Perhaps I'll have time later this week to complete the tour," Malik answered, shadows forming beneath his strong cheekbones. "The palace is a thousand years old. Countless artisans have devoted their lives to embellishing the palace's natural beauty.'' He then nodded at the others, indicating that Fatima and his advisors were to continue on.

Malik waited until the others had disappeared before continuing. Some of his formality eased. ''You could be comfortable here then?''

''How could I not be? You've thought of every comfort imaginable.''

His eyes warmed, the silver glints brightening. ''And I have quite an imagination.''

Nic knew he wasn't just speaking of creature comforts now, and again she felt as if she'd stumbled into another world, one existing just for King Nuri and her. Their conversations had become increasingly private, their references more personal, their innuendos more blatant.

''I'm sure you have a good imagination,'' Nic agreed with mock seriousness. ''Most men think they've a good imagination.''

''You doubt my imagination?''

''I'm certain you are imaginative...for a man—''

''Double standards?''

''Of course.''

He shook his head. ''You're forcing me to respond to your challenge.''

She tried to keep a straight face. ''I'm not challenging you, Your Highness, I'm simply stating a fact.''

''A fact?''

''Yes. Most men think they know what women want, and women need—''

''Oh dear, another problematic declaration.'' He folded his arms across his chest. ''I had no idea you were so chauvinistic.''

''I'm not.''

''Indeed, you are.'' He held up a hand, his gesture imperial. ''But unlike you, I do not endlessly engage in debate. Words accomplish nothing. I, personally, prefer action.''

Her breath felt trapped inside her lungs. She could barely nod. ''Yes.''

''Good.'' And moving forward, he clasped her face in his hands and tilted her face up to his.

The way his fingers splayed across her jawbone, the slow

caress of his thumb beneath her lower lip, the shrewd expression in his eyes sent a shiver through her. Expectation. Desire. *He was going to kiss her.*

Then his head descended and he did kiss her—slowly, curiously, as if he'd wondered for quite a long time what this kiss would feel like, as if the kiss was crucial to some little part of the universe.

Her mouth softened beneath the pressure of his, her lips parting ever so slightly at the tingling pressure. Malik smelled of cedar and cardamom, sweet, spicy. His lips were cool and firm and she felt helplessly fascinated by the slow sensual questing of his lips against hers. He wasn't directing, commanding, demanding. He was simply touching her, letting her experience…him.

And it was unbelievable. He—like the kiss—was warm, sensual, fragrant, her body responded by softening, sending sharp sparkly darts through her belly, to her breasts, and between her thighs. She hadn't felt longing like this in ages. She actually clenched her knees, surprised by the waves of tension and sensation, pleasure and expectation.

Malik trailed one hand down her cheek, his fingers cupping her ear, skimming her cheek and she opened her mouth in a silent gasp. He was doing everything right, *too* right.

Heart hammering, she broke away, took a quick, unsteady step backwards. "Not bad." Her voice came out breathless, high. "For a start."

His expression mocked her. Heat glowed in his eyes, along with a measure of confidence. "You want more."

"That's not what I said—"

"But you want more."

Arrogant man, she thought, and yet he had a right to be. His kiss had melted her bones, turned her into a shivering bundle of need. "I wouldn't be adverse to—" and she drew a quick breath to steady the pounding of her heart "—challenging my assumptions."

"We shall see what we can do." He smiled. "But unfortunately we have business first. You're aware of tonight's reception? It's a political affair."

She nodded, head still spinning a little. "I'll be meeting your cabinet members, and their wives."

"I want them to like you, Princess."

Her eyes locked with his. "Is it important that they do?"

"No." And he dropped his head, kissed her on the corner of her mouth and whispered, "I just want them to like you as much as I do."

Back in her own suite of rooms, Nicolette trembled as she sat in the deep steaming bath, emotions still running high, tension rippling through. Malik's parting words, spoken in his sexy, husky voice, had shaken her nearly as much as the kiss.

He liked her. Not because she was a European princess. Not because she represented a powerful alliance. He liked her because he liked *her*.

And that alone made her happy. She'd no intention of becoming anyone's wife, but she was quite curious about King Nuri—in and out of bed.

Nic could hear Alea in the next room, humming as she laid out Nic's clothes for the state reception. Would Malik kiss her again later? Would they even be alone later?

Nicolette thought she could endure just about anything at the dinner if it meant she'd have ten minutes alone with Malik.

No, ten minutes wouldn't do.

An hour. A solid hour of uninterrupted time alone.

It'd been months and months since she felt anything remotely this strong. Years since she'd had a really satisfying love affair. Years ago, she'd had a fantastic lover, and he'd ruined her for all others. A man that couldn't use his hands, his mouth, his sense of touch wasn't a man at all. It wasn't enough to be physically endowed. A man had to know how to please a woman, although most men thought if they just kept thrusting long enough they'd reached the goal. Problem was, most women needed a hell of a lot more than that. But try telling that to a man.

Even playboys, rich gorgeous, sexy playboys didn't know what turned on a woman most of the time. Fortunately, Malik didn't seem to fall into that category. His brief kiss, his tantalizing caress, conveyed a world of knowledge and experience she was anxious to try.

Alea's footsteps sounded on the marble floor as she made her way through the bedchamber to the walk-in closet across from the bath. Nic could hear her sorting through hanging clothes in the closet.

"Yellow or green?" The young assistant called to Nicolette. "Two dresses arrived earlier this afternoon."

Nic swiped at the steaming water, the jasmine scented bath oil forming smaller pools on the surface. "They're not for the wedding?"

"Oh, no, Princess. You will have special gown for wedding. These are just for you to look beautiful."

"Which do you like better?" Nic asked, content to have the decision made. Some things she fought for. Some things she delegated. Fashion she delegated.

"The green, I think. The color will look striking with your lovely dark hair."

Her dark hair. Nic suddenly sat up, touched the top of her head where her hair had been pinned up on extra large Velcro rollers. Brunette. She was a brunette. It still seemed strange to think she'd gone dark.

Would she ever become blonde Nic Ducasse again?

Four hours later, the long dinner had ended, and instead of providing entertainment, King Nuri had encouraged his guests to mingle—a decidedly Western approach—but one he hoped would give Nicolette a chance to meet more of his cabinet members. But looking at her now, cornered by a dozen robed ladies—including his cousin Fatima—Malik realized he'd made a tactical error.

Nic wasn't getting a chance to meet anyone. The women were keeping her firmly sequestered in the corner. Men on one side of the room, ladies on the other. Malik could imagine the topics the women would be discussing, too. Conversation would be limited to domestic events—marriage, childbirth, health of the elders. There'd be talk about servants, discussion about the cost of food, complaints that the weather was unusually hot and yet it was too early for everyone to trek to summer homes.

Nic made a gesture, and slight bow, indicating she was about to leave the others when Fatima touched Nic's arm in a silent reprimand.

Malik stopped listening to the conversation around him and watched his cousin speak to Nicolette.

Fatima tended to be overly harsh with Nicolette.

Malik knew Fatima didn't understand why he'd chosen a woman like Nicolette, or why he'd go so far from their culture for the woman who would be his mate, his wife, who would bear his children. Baraka's heirs.

But he knew what she did not—he needed someone like her.

Nic would teach their sons and daughters to set goals, to dream big, to fight for what one believed.

It was what all children should be taught, he thought, watching Fatima's face tighten with irritation. She was angry with Nicolette for being different than Barakan women, and yet Fatima had been given opportunities to travel, to live abroad, to find a more Western husband. But Fatima didn't want to leave Atiq. She was waiting, she said, for the right man.

His lashes lowered as he watched Nic turn away, focus on an object beyond her shoulder and he realized that Nicolette was struggling to conceal her anger. What had Fatima said now?

Suddenly Nic turned her head and looked at him. Her blue gaze met his. The corner of her mouth pulled and her expression turned wry.

Save me, her expression seemed to say. And yet she wasn't complaining. She was half amused, half resigned. The not-so-storybook-life of a modern princess.

It was obvious she'd been through this before, many, many times. The princess at a state dinner. The princess, guest of honor at a charity ball, princess, keynote speaker at a fund-raiser.

She might be the family rebel—she might have covered up her gorgeous blond hair with a horrible brown hair dye—but she never shirked her duties.

She might think she wasn't a proper princess, but she understood family and loyalty, she understood what it was to protect and honor.

She'd make a perfect queen. Little did she know that by taking Chantal's place, Nic had given Malik everything he ever wanted in a bride.

Malik made his way across the room and the ladies surrounding Nicolette bowed and parted, leaving him alone with his betrothed.

"Enjoying yourself?" he asked, seeing that Fatima alone stayed at Nic's side.

Nicolette shot him an exasperated glance. "It's a fine party." Her lips pursed. "If you're eighty."

So she was bored. "Too slow for your tastes?"

"Your Highness, no one is doing anything."

"And what would you like to do?"

"Real conversation wouldn't hurt, or maybe turn on some music and let people dance."

He shook his head regretfully. "We can't dance in mixed company." Then he smiled. "But you and your ladies could dance if we men excused ourselves."

"Dance with women?"

He liked the way her cheeks darkened. Nic didn't blush very often and the pink was most becoming, especially tonight in her lime green gown, the color deliciously cool on her lightly tanned skin, making her look as if she were a mouth watering sorbet. "Of course. Dancing with women can be quite exciting."

The silver charm bracelet on her wrist tinkled as she gestured displeasure. "Your Highness, I don't dance with other women."

"It's not a slow dance with women. It's a fast dance. Energetic." He was trying hard not to laugh at her hand hovering before her mouth, her blue eyes wide and indignant. "The dance gets your heart pumping, your body moving."

"Aerobics?"

"Think of it as an Arabic version of Jazzercise." He saw her incredulous expression. "I know what Jazzercise is. One of my sisters lives in San Francisco. She loves her aerobic classes—"

Nicolette started to laugh. She tried to stifle the sound by covering her mouth but it didn't work. The more she tried to stop laughing, the harder she laughed. Tears filled her eyes. She wheezed behind her hand. "That's priceless."

Fatima looked on in horror but Malik found Nic's laughter sexy…refreshing. Nic had laughed with her whole face. Her laughter was contagious and it healed something in him that had been damaged from the attempt on his life a year ago.

He needed to laugh. He needed to feel hope. Nicolette gave him hope, and wasn't hope a wonderful thing?

He leaned toward her, preventing his cousin from hearing his words. "We could always leave," he murmured. "I'm sure we could find some diversions back at the palace."

CHAPTER SIX

HEAT flared in Nic's eyes. Her soft lush lips parted and his own body instantly hardened. He knew exactly what she was thinking. He was thinking the very same thing.

When he kissed her earlier, he hoped to contain his attraction, curtail some of his less inhibited thoughts, but the kiss did nothing to quiet his imagination. He'd thought of nothing but her since then. Wanted nothing but her beneath him, against him, above him.

When would he be able to take her to his bed? Make love to her properly?

Not while they were here, that was for certain.

First they had to get through their goodbyes, and it took a good ten minutes, but they were finally finished and escaping to the car when Fatima appeared and asked for a return ride home.

Nic groaned inwardly. She'd been thrilled at the idea of a long private drive home. Now the long drive would be anything but relaxing, or private.

The three settled into the back of Malik's waiting limousine, Fatima and Nicolette on one side, the sultan on the other.

"Glad to be gone, Princess?" Malik asked, as the limousine pulled away from the state building.

"I was tired tonight," Nicolette admitted with a small sigh. She'd felt off balance tonight, not quite herself. It was the newness of everything, she tried to tell herself, the different food, the different language and customs. But deep down she knew her headache was due to adrenaline. Her body felt hot, sensitive, her pulse quick like an engine revved.

He'd started something with that kiss. Now she just wanted him to finish it.

In the dim light of the interior Malik smiled briefly, acknowledging her honesty. "Do you find it difficult being the only foreigner in the room?"

Nic plucked at her green silk sleeve, letting the weight of the cool silver beads fall against the back of her hand. "I'm accustomed to being the only foreigner at state events. But I have to admit, tonight I did feel…different."

"*You* are different," Fatima interrupted. "You don't dress like women in Baraka, you prefer not to robe and veil yourself—"

"I've never asked her to, either," Malik quietly reproved his cousin. "Princess Ducasse is entitled to be herself here."

"Then how can she be a proper queen if she isn't a role model?" Fatima flashed.

"Enough," he answered, curtly. "This is not your concern."

Fatima dropped her head, but Nicolette saw the anger flare in Fatima's eyes. Nic struggled to think of something to say. What could she say? She and Fatima had had a rocky relationship from the very first meeting.

The limousine wound through the quiet city streets, turning from one wide palm-lined boulevard onto another. Minutes passed in silence. The air conditioner blew, a quiet hum of artificially chilled air. Nic adjusted her delicate wrap, covering her shoulders more thoroughly.

"Is the air too cool?" Malik asked.

"It's fine, thank you," Nic answered, touched by his concern. "It feels good after the warmth of the party."

"I was warm, too," he said, and then paused, his attention focused on her. Nic felt his interest, his gaze resting on her face, or what he could see in the flashing light and shadows. "Our older buildings were designed with high ceilings to draw the warm air up, but the newer government buildings lack adequate ventilation."

Nic smiled deprecatingly. "I think all government buildings are identical. Perhaps they share the same architect?"

"Or same sensibilities," he agreed.

Fatima sighed heavily and stirred, and Nic fell silent, self-conscious all over again.

Malik ignored his cousin. "Tell me, Chantal," and his deep voice was like velvet against her senses—his timbre, rich, sensual, impossibly male. "When you're queen, what is the first thing you'll do?"

* * *

Nicolette wished Fatima were not here, hanging on to every word. "Do you mean as in programs?" she asked, thinking about all the causes near and dear to her family's heart back in Melio.

"Programs, issues, activities. I'm just curious to know what you'd care about as queen. How you'd spend your time and energy here."

Nic had her causes, too, and since discovering the extent of Chantal's misery in La Croix, Nicolette had taken it upon herself to set up women's centers on each of the islands in Melio where women could ask questions, request help, even seek refuge.

She'd do the same thing here, too. She'd want to do something for women. It'd stunned her that Chantal had been physically abused, but now that Nicolette's eyes were opened, she was determined to reach as many women as she could. If Chantal had suffered in such silence, God only knows the number of women in need. The number of women not helped.

"I'd like to help women," Nicolette answered evenly, knowing that Malik was now aware of Chantal's wretched life in La Croix. "I have the name, the visibility, and the connections— all I lack is the means."

"Which you won't lack as Queen of Baraka."

Nic thought of the women living in Baraka who might be in desperate need of a helping hand. If she as Queen couldn't make a change for the better, then who could?

But you won't be queen, she reminded herself. This is just a game…

But it didn't feel like a game anymore. Not at all.

She slowly peeled off her long pale green evening gloves. Everything about her life here felt real. Her emotions, her hopes, her worries.

"How would you begin?" Malik persisted, apparently genuinely interested in wanting to hear more.

"Education." Nic lay the satin gloves on top of her small beaded purse. Chantal would never support this issue though. Chantal couldn't fight for herself, much less anyone else. "I'd want to improve education for girls—"

"Our education here is excellent," Fatima interrupted. "Girls are treated very well in Baraka. The majority attend school."

"Yes, you did, Fatima," Nicolette answered gently. "You

hold a college degree, and your parents supported your educational pursuit, but that's not the norm for poorer families, is it?'' Nic didn't wait for Fatima to answer. ''If I were queen, I'd like to see all children in school until seventeen, and I'd want to encourage girls to continue to college and vocational programs so that every girl has a choice in life, opportunity—''

Fatima snapped her fingers. ''They *have* a choice. They can choose marriage, they aren't married against their will. Parents and matchmakers consult daughters here. We are not barbaric like some countries. And a wife and mother is always loved.''

As if saying yes or no to an arranged spouse was freedom of choice!

Nic said nothing for a long moment then shook her head. ''There are many ways of being loved. Women should at least have the option to choose how they are loved, and that includes choosing career or home. Women shouldn't be home because they have no other choice, but because it's the place they choose to be. The path they seek.''

''And you, Princess Chantal,'' Malik interjected kindly, diffusing some of the tension, ''are you doing what you want to be? Have you found your path?''

Nicolette met his gaze in the shadows of the car. Ah, tricky question. Had she found her path?

No.

Had she ever tried to find her path before?

No.

Why?

''I think I'm still searching,'' she said after a moment, feeling foolish, aware of Fatima's seething animosity.

''So what are you searching for?'' His question was maddeningly simple.

Nic flashed back to the palace in Melio, her elderly grandparents, her sisters gathered in her bedroom, all of them sprawled on her bed talking about the future, what needed to be done for the future of their country. ''Me,'' she whispered.

Fatima snorted in disgust. ''Typical Western answer,'' she muttered, turning her head away, staring pointedly out the car window.

Heat burned through Nic, a blush flooding her face. Me, she

silently mocked herself. Me, had been such a self-absorbed answer. A childish concept.

Searching for oneself.

Trying to find oneself.

"We're all called to search for the truth," Malik said, and she looked up to find that his expression had gentled, and there was compassion in his cool silver gaze. "Without self-knowledge, we are nothing. If we do not know ourselves, we can not love ourselves, or anyone else for that matter."

Nic's eyes suddenly watered. She bent her head, focused on the pair of pale green gloves draped across her small evening purse, telling herself that no matter what, she couldn't, wouldn't, cry in front of Fatima. "Thank you."

Arriving back at the palace, Malik didn't have to walk Nicolette back to her rooms, but he insisted, and she was glad. Well, sort of glad. Her heart felt very heavy at the moment and things she thought she could do, things she thought she could ignore, weren't quite so cut and dry anymore.

She was deceiving a man she greatly admired.

The quiet of the palace, and the spots of moonlight shimmering on the marble floor wrapped around Nicolette, making her feel truly lonely for the first time since she arrived.

"Do you ever wonder if perhaps you have the wrong sister?" she asked softly, her voice barely audible.

Malik glanced down at her, his expression one of concern. "Do you think I have the wrong sister?"

"I just wonder if perhaps I'm not really the one you want…"

His brow furrowed. "In terms of outlook? Attitude?"

Her shoulders lifted, fell, the silk of her gown sliding across her skin. "I don't know. Maybe I'm confused why you picked me. Why not one of the others?"

They'd reached her suite of rooms and stood outside her door. "I suppose I could have proposed to Joelle instead," he said, rubbing his jaw.

"Joelle?" Why Joelle? She's barely an adult. "She's too young for you."

"Perhaps you're too old for me."

Nic felt her cheeks burn. "You're at least ten years older than me, King Nuri."

"But let's be honest, Chantal, shall we? I'm excited about

marriage and the possibility of having a family. You, forgive me, seem so blasé about it all. I would rather have a young bride eager to experience marriage and motherhood than a wife that dreads matrimony.''

"Yet there are three Ducasse princesses. You haven't mentioned Nicolette.''

He waved a hand, brushing aside the suggestion. "She was never an option.''

"Why not?''

Another impatient gesture. "She's not suitable—''

"Why not?''

He gave her a sharp look. "If this is upsetting you, we ought not continue the discussion.''

"It is upsetting me, and we should continue the conversation because I want to understand. Nicolette's much beloved by her people—''

"Yes, but to be Queen Nuri, queen of Baraka, one must be more than great, one must be above reproach.''

Apparently Chantal hadn't been exaggerating when she'd said that Nic's reputation was destroying her chances of a good marriage. "Yet you've never even met her. How can you be so critical?''

He didn't look the least bit apologetic. "It's common knowledge that she prefers playboys and libertines.''

Playboys? *"Libertines?''*

"She's not a virgin.''

Nic flushed hotly. "Neither am I.''

"But you were when you married.''

Nic squeezed the gloves into a ball in her hand. And Joelle was still innocent. Damn him. What was wrong with a woman experimenting a little? Figuring out what she wanted…needed? Why could a man do what he wanted but a woman had to worry about reputation? "You're not a virgin.''

His lips curved but he wasn't smiling. "It's a man's duty to know how to pleasure his wife.''

"And a woman has no need to know how to pleasure a man?''

"Her husband will teach her.''

"That's absurd!''

"Why?''

She thought of poor Chantal, married off as a twenty-two year old virgin to a man who didn't give a fig for her happiness, or comfort, and who most certainly didn't bother to educate her in the art of love. Nic was certain that Chantal had never had an orgasm in her life—and if she'd had—it was probably alone. "My late husband taught me nothing."

"Then he failed in his duty."

"Just as I am quite certain that many men then 'fail in their duty.' Most men still have no concept where the clitoris is let alone how to touch it!"

His stunned silence said more than words ever could. Nic realized she'd said far, far too much and she gripped her gloves so tightly she felt frozen in place.

Why was she so intent on changing his opinion about "Nicolette"? What did it matter if he disapproved of her? Let him think what he wanted to think. It was foolish and irresponsible to let her ego get the better of her. She had to protect Chantal. She had to play Chantal until she'd gotten word that Lilly was safe.

"I said too much," she said, swallowing hard, realizing she was swallowing her pride.

But he said nothing.

She'd have to apologize again. "I was wrong, Malik. I'm sorry. I shouldn't have been so...detailed."

"I didn't realize you'd had so much experience."

"I'm a woman. I have friends. Sisters—"

"Nicolette."

He'd said her name so disapprovingly that it made her stomach free fall. "You really don't like her."

"I don't know her."

Nic nodded painfully, her face still scalding hot, more from anger than shame.

After he'd left, Nic let herself into her suite of rooms, and with her insides still churning with resentment, she changed into her pajamas, and then wandered outside. Trying to calm herself, she walked the length of her private courtyard with the deep still pool and the fountain with the beautiful marble statue.

It was late out, but the night was still hot, and the sultry night air hung on her, making her want to turn around and retreat to the cool dark suite. But she couldn't go inside. She felt even more trapped inside. Scared, too.

Malik occupied her thoughts lately—endlessly. She wanted to pretend it was mere curiosity, cultural fascination, even sexual infatuation, but deep down she knew her interest was so much more than that.

He was an ideal ruler for a country like Baraka where the culture dated back thousands of years and people had been forced to reinvent themselves following earthquakes, fires, tragedies.

And God knows she didn't want to shame him, not in front of his people. Not in front of the world. And certainly not in private, either.

How on earth was she going to extricate herself from this? It would be one thing if he liked Princess Nicolette. It would ease some of her guilt and misery. But he didn't like Nicolette. He'd been most clear from the beginning that he would not, could not make Nicolette Ducasse his queen.

So maybe there lay the solution to her problem.

If she didn't want to embarrass him by breaking the engagement, she'd force him into taking action. She'd continue the masquerade as long as necessary, and then, once Lilly was safe, Nic would she reveal the shocking truth—that she was really that blonde, shallow, wanton princess he so despised.

He'd never marry her then.

Nic crossed her arms over her chest and tipped her head back to take in the dark purplish sky and bit her lip to keep from crying.

She couldn't cry. For heaven's sake! She wasn't here to find true love. She was here to get a job done.

It's a job, she reminded herself, crawling into bed. She was helping those who needed her most.

Early the next morning Fatima was admitted to Malik's office and seeing him still on the phone, she took a seat on a low chair in the corner and waited patiently for him to finish his conversation.

When he finally hung up, he looked up at her. He was wearing a pair of dark framed reading glasses. "Do you know why I wanted to see you?"

Fatima's tranquil expression betrayed nothing. "You will tell me, I am sure."

He studied his cousin a long moment. Fatima had taken an almost immediate dislike to Nicolette and he still hadn't figured out if it was jealousy, insecurity or something deeper. "I've felt your hostility to our guest."

Fatima didn't even blink. "She's not going to marry you, cousin."

"Not if you continue to intimidate her."

Fatima lifted her right hand, a gentle dismissal. "I am being truthful with her, and with you. I do not trust her, Malik. She's playing you."

One of his black eyebrows arched slightly. He barely glanced her way. "That's an awfully Western expression coming from you."

"I've been to the West, I've lived in the West, I understand Western culture as well as you do." Fatima shook her head soberly. "Malik. Listen to me." She stared at him pointedly, one of those dagger sharp stares that is next to impossible to ignore.

He met her gaze, her dark eyes unsmiling. "Listen to me, cousin," she added flatly, no urgency in her voice, just conviction. "She's. Not. Going. To. Marry. You."

Malik pulled off his reading glasses and dropped them on his desk, rubbing his eyes as he did so. "Why not?"

"She's too independent. She's not interested in our country, or culture, and quite honestly, I don't think she's all that interested in you."

Malik frowned, partially agreeing with her, partially disagreeing knowing that Fatima had always been bright, but she didn't know about chemistry, or attraction. She had no concept about physical desire, and when it came to physical desire, the princess was very attracted to him. Nic might not want to marry him, but she definitely was interested in being intimate with him.

"I'm not worried," he said rising from his chair and moving toward Fatima. "She needs me," he said, standing over his cousin. "Her country needs what I can offer."

Fatima shook her head. "But what if she gets just enough from you that she doesn't need the rest? What if she needs less than you think she does?"

Good point. Fatima had always been smart. She'd excelled in school. She could have done anything with her life, but she'd chosen to remain here, at the palace. What would she do with her life, he'd often wondered. A member of the royal family, she was worth a fortune and with her father dead, her mother living in New York, she belonged beneath his protection. Who would ever be good enough for her?

"I'll have to be careful then, won't I?" he answered evenly, and then he smiled at her. She was beautiful. Dark eyes, high cheekbones, firm chin, slightly pointed with masses of long silky black hair. Fatima looked like their grandmother but she had her father's cunning mind. "Now you better go. The princess will be waiting for her language lesson."

Nicolette was waiting in the salon for Fatima, but she wasn't thinking about her lesson. She was thinking that she had the strangest secret. It was her birthday today, her real birthday, but she couldn't celebrate because no one knew who she really was.

It was rather odd thinking she'd reached twenty-seven. Suddenly it seemed like such an old age. Chantal had already been married several years when she turned twenty-seven. So far Nicolette had done...what?

Nothing.

Fatima arrived and the lesson proceeded without incident, and then as the serving girl arrived, bringing the now expected tray of tea and sweet biscuits, the serving girl curtsied to Nicolette. "Princess, His Highness would like you to join him for a late breakfast," the girl said. "I'm to show you the way."

Fatima's face tightened but she didn't protest, and Nicolette followed the serving girl through the corridors and out to one of the gorgeous inner courtyards reserved for the sultan's personal use.

Malik was already at the wrought-iron table that had been set for two. Bright flowers filled a dark green glass vase and Nic decided she'd make this her birthday party. He didn't even need to know it was her birthday. It was enough that she could be with him now, start her day with his company. Already his company meant so much...

"Good morning," Malik greeted, leaning forward to kiss her on each cheek. "I've been thinking of you."

She shivered as his lips grazed her cheek. He smelled lovely.

She wished she could capture his face between her hands and kiss him properly. No more fleeting kisses on the cheeks, but a long, deep kiss, one that would make her melt again. "Have you?"

He leaned forward on the table, his black hair almost glossy in the bright light. "I've also felt very guilty."

"Why?"

"I've been unkind with regards to your sister. I know how I feel about my brother and sisters and wouldn't tolerate anyone speaking harshly about them, and yet I have been incredibly intolerant of Nicolette's idiosyncrasies. Forgive me."

Nic looked away, embarrassed as well as uncomfortable. "She's not really so—eccentric." She'd intended to reply matter of factly, but to her shame, her voice broke. Even when he apologized he made it sound as if Nic was this peculiar woman with cannibalistic tendencies. "Maybe she's not Barakan, but she's good. And kind. And she doesn't say cruel things about people." Nic drew a wobbly breath, shaken. "She doesn't judge people, either. And she wouldn't be here right now, judging you, or judging your cousin Fatima who can't say a nice thing about anyone."

Finished she sat there, words spent, emotion spent, all illusions about a party dashed. It wasn't a fun birthday morning. It was another horrible day living a lie. "Would you excuse me, please?" she whispered.

"No."

His refusal surprised her. She pushed away from the table. He might be king in Baraka, but she was royalty in Europe. "I'd like to return to my lessons with Fatima."

"Even though she's judgmental?"

"I'd rather her be judgmental than *you*."

"Why?"

Tears burned in her eyes and she looked at him so overwhelmed by emotions she hadn't expected to feel that she didn't even think she could find her voice.

"Why?" he demanded yet again.

The rest of Nic's control snapped. "Because I like you. I don't want you to be mean. Or petty. I don't want you to be cruel just because Nicolette isn't your idea of the perfect woman. No one's perfect, King Nûri, and even those of us who aren't perfect, are still pretty worthy of love, and loyalty.''

"I was apologizing—"

"Not really. Not enough." Her lip quivered. She felt so wretched she couldn't even bear it. "It's her birthday today, and I don't think she deserves this—"

"I know it's her birthday!" He nearly shouted, his voice echoing. "That's why you're here with me this morning. I wanted to celebrate with you."

She fought to regain control and her chest rose and fell with each deep shuddering breath. "How did you know it's her birthday? You don't even like her."

He stood, leaned across the table, cupping the back of her head, and kissed her. "Because I like you," he said, kissing her again. "I like you so much I've tried to learn everything I can about your family."

The tears shimmered in her eyes, making it very hard to see, but if she blinked, the tears would fall. "How old is she then?"

"Twenty-seven." He reached up with the tip of her finger and caught the tears clinging to her lower lashes. "And I know you're worried about her because she's getting old and she's still not married—"

Nic batted away with his hand. "She's not that old."

"But she should be married, shouldn't she?"

And to show her he was teasing, he kissed her yet again, a light kiss, but something happened when his lips touched hers this time. The restraint was gone. The pure intentions disappeared. Instead emotion sizzled and the slow, tender kiss blazed into pure, raw, unadulterated desire.

Nic had felt desire, but this desire took her breath away, turned her belly inside out, made her ache with need.

She reached for him, fingers twining in his shirt, and his lips ruthlessly parted hers, his tongue stabbing at the softness of her mouth, tasting, teasing, making her aware that he'd been gentle with her so far, but he could also be fiercely hungry, and demanding.

Nic clung to him, welcoming the intensity, finding release in the violence of emotion. All her life she'd craved passion, and to find it here—and now—with Malik stunned her.

He lifted his head, stroked her cheek. "Forgive me. Please?"

"Of course." And she managed a tremulous smile, something of a feat considering the intense desire still coiling inside her. It hurt to kiss. It hurt even more to end the kiss. She'd never felt so unfulfilled. "And Nic forgives you, too."

"Then we can still have breakfast to celebrate her special day?"

She grinned ruefully. "Yes."

"And can we start over, pretend nothing's happened?"

Her laugh was soft, husky. "Are you that good of an actor?"

"Depends. Are you that good of an actress?"

Nic thought of the past week at the palace. "No." She laughed yet again, making fun of herself. "I'm a terrible actress. I've never been picked to play a lead in any of our school theatre productions."

He held her chair for her, and slid her chair into the table once she was seated. "Not even though you were a very famous princess?"

She made a face. "I'd like to say there was a bias against princesses, but that isn't the case. My sister, Joelle, is a fantastic actress. She also inherited Mom's voice. Joelle's voice is like an angel's. You have to hear her sing one day—" Nic broke off, blushed. "Listen to me. You've turned me into a chatterbox."

He gestured for coffee and a steward instantly appeared, filling their cups. "You're far from a chatterbox, Chantal. I have to work to make you talk."

Nic reached out to touch the floral arrangement, her fingertip brushing across one crimson rose petal. The damask roses in the floral arrangement made the air smell spicy and sweet. "Men like quiet women."

Malik spluttered on his coffee. "I can't believe you say these things."

"At least it makes you smile."

"I'm just glad you're smiling again."

CHAPTER SEVEN

THEIR eyes met and held. Nic saw the sincerity in his lovely silver gaze, and felt little ripples of pleasure hum through her. They were making small talk and yet below the surface the most intense attraction simmered, and the awareness that they both felt so much, fueled the desire.

"So what is on your calendar today?" he asked, sitting back as a serving girl set a plate of fresh sliced, peeled fruits before him—mangos, papayas, kiwi, pomegranate. The colors were vivid, wet, glistening. Like jewels drenched by the rain.

Nic's mouth watered. She was hungry. But not just for food. She wanted his mouth again, wanted his tongue and the spicy taste of his skin.

"It's busy," she answered, knowing perfectly well that her schedule was packed with appointments, including another fitting followed by two hours in the kitchen with the master chef learning about Baraka's cuisine before being given her first instruction in how to prepare the sultan's favorite dishes.

"Perhaps we've kept you too busy. The strain is showing."

She made a wry face. "Apologies, Your Highness."

He smiled. "Do you need a holiday?"

"No books? No activities? No homework? What would I do?" She feigned shock.

"I suppose you'd have to enjoy my company. If such a thing is possible." He speared a circle of kiwi and put it in his mouth, chewing slowly, letting the ripe sweet fruit dissolve even more slowly.

She watched his firm, mobile mouth take the succulent fruit, watched his jaw move once, twice, saw the long strong column of his throat swallow and she exhaled in a tight, thin stream of air. A day alone with Malik wasn't her idea of relaxing. She couldn't relax around him. She'd begun to crave contact with him too badly. "I know you've many state appointments—"

"Too many," he agreed solemnly.

"It wouldn't be fair for me to add to your pressures—"

"But, *laeela*, you must come first. You're to be my queen. My wife. My lover."

Heat surged to Nic's cheeks. *His lover.* And she loved the sound of that word, even as the image conjured up all the press clippings she'd read, the stories of his many mistresses scattered around the world.

She felt his gaze caress her now, sweeping her cheeks, down the column of her throat to rest at her breasts. She was wearing a turquoise silk pantsuit, the collarless jacket conservative by Western standards, and yet his desire made her feel naked. Exposed.

"Yes, well, of course there are the duties," she said hurriedly, "but right now, if you have greater pressing concerns—"

"Greater concerns? Princess, I'd be amiss not to be concerned with you. I can see you are a little lonely today." The smile faded from his eyes. "I can see you are a little sad. I think you need some company. I think you could use me."

Use him. Oh, indeed. She could use him but that wasn't part of the plan.

The plan wasn't to make love.

The plan wasn't to fall in love.

The plan wasn't to get trapped in this country so far away from her own.

"We can always meet later—for dinner." She pressed her knees together, tucking one foot behind the other ankle. She couldn't let herself want more from him. She couldn't continue to let herself get emotionally invested. "You can tell me what you've done…"

Her voice faded as Malik leaned forward and ran the pad of his thumb over her lips, silencing her. "You need an adventure today. Something new, something fun. Leave it to me."

"Malik."

"Yes, *laeela?*"

Her eyes burned and she closed her eyes as his hand slid along her jaw, and down, along the side of her neck to rest at her collarbone. His fingers were so sure and steady against her warm bare skin that Nic found the lovely sensation almost too excruciating to enjoy.

"Why don't you ever look me in the eye?" he asked softly, the pad of his thumb stroking the hollow of her throat. "When we talk like this, you always look away."

"You're touching me," she whispered, and he was right, she couldn't meet his gaze. He'd stirred intense emotions in her, and even hotter desire, and the combination of the two tried her conscience.

Her heart ached almost constantly and her body felt restless, a ceaseless restlessness that came from wanting.

But the wanting was reckless, dangerous, and even Nic, who embraced danger knew what was at stake here.

Chantal and Lilly.

"My touch shouldn't frighten you," Malik said. "You're not a virgin, not without experience."

She swallowed, her skin flaming with heat, her belly heavy, empty. "It's not lack of experience that makes me wary, and it's not your touch I fear." She looked up into his perceptive pewter gaze. "What I fear is...you."

"You fear me?" He sounded incredulous. "But why? I'd protect you with my life."

Nicolette's heart twisted. The pain startled her. She hadn't felt such strong emotion in years. "Maybe that's what I'm afraid of." Jaw pressed tight, she gazed intently at his hard features, the long aquiline nose, the broad jaw, the stubborn set of his chin. "You place too much trust in me. You haven't known me long enough to offer your life in exchange of mine."

His palm suddenly cupped her cheek. "But you're my betrothed."

"We haven't exchanged any words, had a formal declaration."

"You are here."

Tears thickened her voice, tears she wasn't going to cry. "But appearances can be deceptive."

His expression turned thoughtful as he sat back in his chair. "Are you thinking of leaving?"

"No."

"But you still have doubts?"

She hated talking like this. Now that she'd met him, gotten to know him she didn't want to be the one to disappoint him. "I was born with doubts. Of the three of us, I was the princess most likely to—'' She broke off, realizing she was about to make another Nicolette pronouncement, and he was suspicious of those Nicolette pronouncements.

"To?" he prompted softly.

"You don't want to know."

"I do."

She shrugged helplessly, as if to say, I warned you. "Most likely to initiate world war."

He coughed.

She flexed her fingers, tension coiling throughout her body. "I know. I'm sorry."

"What can we do? How can I help?" He sounded so tranquil, so comfortably conversational. "Is there something that I could do? Something I could tell you?"

She closed her eyes, felt the late morning sun warm the top of her head, wrap her shoulders in heat. She didn't know what she was doing anymore. Didn't know how she'd lost control of the situation. She wasn't supposed to get involved here. She was to have been a guest…just a guest… Instead she'd started to feel things, genuine things, for Malik Nuri.

Nic swallowed, opened her eyes. Malik should have been troubled but he looked calm, as if all his concern was for her instead of himself. "I don't want to—" her mouth had gone dry and she reached for her glass of juice, took a sip, wetting her lips "—humiliate you."

"I'm glad. I hate being humiliated." But the corner of his lips lifted, and he sounded downright cavalier.

She didn't know how he could joke at a time like this, yet she smiled at his humor, her emotions strung up like the rope of flags on the *Royal Star*.

"But you're not going to humiliate me," he continued confidently. "I know you. You're like me. You understand duty, and responsibility. You love your country, your people, and your family. You'll do what's best for them."

He was speaking matter of factly and she found herself hanging on each word, as if she couldn't wait to hear what he'd say next. "If you give me your word now," he added, "I know the ceremony will take place. You wouldn't cancel at the last minute, now when it'd be so awkward for both our families. Never mind national pride."

National pride. Nic couldn't speak, couldn't make a sound, and life seemed to crystallize around her—the sun shining through her glass, filling the guava juice with shimmering light, the heady scent of the damask roses, the forlorn cry of a seagull above, a reminder that the Atlantic sea wasn't so very far away.

"You're free," he added even more gently. "You're free to go home now. I'd never keep you here against your will."

He didn't even know who she was, she thought, and if she did marry him, pretending to be Chantal, what would happen later when he found out later she wasn't Chantal? Would he say fine, one Ducasse is the same as another, or would he want Chantal—the good one—the obedient one, and divorce her on grounds of fraud? Deception?

But if Nic confessed the truth now, what would happen to Chantal and Lilly? What if they were close to getting home to Melio? What if Nicolette ruined it for them now?

She couldn't imagine that all this…subterfuge…should be for naught.

"I'm not going anywhere." Her voice sounded rough. "I'm staying right here." Nic looked up at him and prayed he wouldn't see the tears in her eyes. "I'm on holiday today, remember? And you've promised me to show me something new…something fun."

"I remember."

After the meal, Nicolette quickly changed shoes, applied some sunscreen to her face and returned to the front hall. Her heart felt heavy when she saw Fatima waiting.

Fatima looked at her. "This wasn't my idea," she said stiffly.

Nic could barely nod, ridiculously disappointed. Just then the car and driver pulled to the door and Malik arrived. Like Fatima, he'd changed into a *jellaba,* and like his cousin, his long robe was made of expensive fabric with ornate needlework lining the seams.

"Do I need to change?" Nic asked, touching the neckline of her turquoise jacket.

"I have a *jellaba* you can wear if you'd like," Malik answered, lightly circling her with his arm. "But I see no need for you to change. You'll find that many of our young people favor jeans and T-shirts. Between our French colonial past, and the flood of tourists in winter, you'll find that our city center is quite Western.''

"Is that where we're going?" she asked, settling into the back seat.

He suddenly spoke in Arabic to his cousin, and Fatima, who'd just sat down next to Nic, reluctantly moved, relocating herself to the opposite seat. Malik took the vacated space next to Nic.

"Is this proper?" Nic whispered to Malik as the king stretched an arm across the back of the seat, his fingertips brushing her shoulder.

"It's my car," he answered, looking down at her.

"Yes, but your cousin—"

"Knows you're to be my wife." He reached for her hand, kissed the back of it. "Now relax. I want you to enjoy yourself. You're not allowed to worry."

"Not about anything?"

"About nothing. Not even Lilly. I've everything under control."

Something in his tone made the fine hair lift at the nape of her neck but she didn't dare ask. He'd said not to worry, and for one hour, she could try to do that much, couldn't she?

With a small convoy of police escorts, the limousine wound through numerous avenues, the streets growing narrower with each turn until they'd reached the market square.

Merchants and peddlers had filled the square with colorful bazaars, their booths offering every kind of ware imaginable. Baskets mounded with fruits and nuts. Copper pots. Bolts of fabric. Leather goods.

Nic sat forward on her seat, anxious to see everything. Malik's fingers trailed down her spine until his hand settled in the small of her back. "You're eager to explore."

She couldn't contain her curiosity. She loved getting out, doing things. It'd been hard being so cooped up in the palace during the past week. "I am."

The driver parked and the security circled the limousine. Malik climbed out, extended a hand to Nicolette and then Fatima.

As Nicolette stood, she realized that nearly all of the women bustling around the market were wearing the long colorful *jellaba.* "Do you still have the…coverall?" she asked, indicating his jellaba. "I think Fatima and I would draw less attention if we looked the same."

Fatima aided Nicolette in settling the long navy *jellaba* over Nic's head, covering her pantsuit.

"Would you care to have a look around?" Malik asked Nic once she was finished dressing.

"Yes," Nic answered, ready to see as much of the medina as she could. She'd wanted to visit the city hub ever since she arrived.

"Fatima will walk with you," he said. "I'd like to go with you, but I think it's less complicated for security if I wait here."

She understood, especially as the market was very crowded and it'd be difficult for a group—much less the sultan and his escorts—to pass through the congested square.

As she and Fatima set off, the sun shone high above, and a hot wind kicked up dust, tugged at the crisp canvas awnings, blowing the palm trees dense green fronds. Nic was nearly overwhelmed by such exotic beauty—the blue and white striped stalls, the massive clay pots of pink and green olives, baskets piled high with dried dates and apricots, the pervasive spice of peppers, and all the while the hot wind brushing and whipping the fronds so the very air seemed to whisper.

Exquisite, she thought, taking it all in, savoring all that was new and mysterious.

"*Balek!*" a man shouted, lumbering past with a cart full of goods.

Balek. Nic smiled. Watch yourself. She'd understood the Arabic word.

Contented, Nic followed Fatima around the parameter of the bustling square, the old buildings fronted by hundreds of souks, each one selling something different, just as each merchant sized the shopper up, setting new and different prices.

Now and then she stopped to examine intriguing merchandise and gradually Nic forgot Fatima's hostility, losing herself in the pleasure of being somewhere altogether new.

As she moved slowly from one seller to another, the sun beat down on her head, the rays penetrating her dark *jellaba*. Time to turn back, she thought. But looking up, hoping to catch Fatima's eye, Nic realized she'd lost Malik's cousin somewhere along the way. Surprised, but not distressed, Nic actually felt…relief. She'd been in many foreign countries, traveled a great deal. It didn't cross her mind to feel fear. Instead, for one brief moment, she felt free. No Fatima, no sultan, no marriage, no worries.

And with that thought in mind, she wished she had money on her and she'd find a café somewhere and buy an iced coffee and just sit in the shade and watch everyone. Atiq was amazing and Nic loved the medina, responding to the history of the inner city with the cobbled streets, whitewashed buildings and dazzling sunlight.

A hand touched her arm and Nic turned. An older woman stood before her, the woman's gray hair partially covered with a long scarf. "Lost?" The elderly woman asked.

Nic smiled. "A little."

The woman stared up at Nic for a minute, her dark eyes puzzled. "You are a very beautiful lady," she said in her halting English.

"Thank you. *Merci,*" Nic answered, switching to French hoping it'd be easier for the older woman. "That's lovely of you to say"

The woman smiled gratefully. "You're not American?" she asked in French.

"No."

The older woman's mouth pursed as she studied Nic's face. "French?"

"Half." Quarter, actually. Julien, her father had been half-French, half-Spanish.

Suddenly the old woman wagged her finger. Her frown faded as she smiled, deep lines creasing her skin. "I know who you look like." She beamed wider. "The American singer. Star."

Star. Mom. And Nic could see her mother, long dark hair, flashing eyes, a wicked sense of humor.

"You know who I'm talking about?" The woman clasped Nic's arm. "Superstar. Married a Spanish prince."

But Mom didn't marry a Spanish prince. He was a Melian prince. Her eyes felt gritty and she blinked, blaming the hot wind. "Thank you."

She patted the older woman's hand where it rested on her arm, the elderly woman's fingers thin, the skin delicate. "I'm very flattered, and you are very kind."

The woman beamed wider, spaces showing between her bottom teeth and reached up to pat Nic's cheek. *"Allah ihennik."* *God make you safe.*

Nic's heart squeezed. A lump filled her throat. "And you," she murmured as the elderly woman shuffled away. She watched the elderly woman fade into the crowd.

It'd been years since anyone said she looked like her mother. With her blonde hair, the family always said she was like Julien, but Nic remembered when she was little, her mother used to sit Nic on her lap and comb her long hair and point to their reflections in the mirror. "You have Mommy's eyes," her mother would say, drawing the boar bristle brush through Nic's curls. "And you have Mommy's mouth and chin."

"And Mommy's nonsense," her father called to them from the bedroom where he'd inevitably be sitting in a chair, or lying in bed, with a stack of state documents. Her father was always reading, preparing, studying up on economies, politics, world events. No one cared more about the future than Prince Julien Ducasse.

It was odd, Nic thought, setting off, threading her way through the crowd, but when her parents died everyone talked about what a tragedy it was, what a loss of beautiful young glamorous people. And beauty was all very nice and fine, but beauty wasn't their strength. Their strength had been their intelligence, their spirit, their drive. Both her father and her mother were real people, not glossy paper dolls, or coat hangers for expensive couture.

What a gift that elderly woman had given her today, what a lovely birthday gift. To be told she looked like her mother. To have a stranger stop her and say I see Star in you…

Nic closed her eyes, pressed her hands to her heart, held all the emotion and welling of love inside.

Now it was time to get back to Malik before he started worrying, and rounding a corner lined with narrow stalls, Nicolette glanced around, sensing she hadn't gone in the right direction. Where had she made a wrong turn? Nothing looked familiar, but then, the maze of merchants and crowded souks was enough to disorient anyone.

Standing at the corner, hands on hips, Nic became aware that she was drawing attention. Women avoided her but men were curious. It was obvious she was a foreigner, and even though she was wearing a traditional coverall, she stood out as different.

Where was she? Where was the central market?

What would Malik say when he found out she'd lost Fatima and was wandering somewhere inside the endless medina?

Nic moved toward a woman to ask for directions but the woman drew her scarf closer to her face and hurried on.

Nic wrinkled her nose. That was not the response she wanted. Glancing left, and then right, the streets much narrower than they had been earlier. What she needed to do was backtrack…

Nic set off again, returning the way she'd come, but the street didn't lead to the market. Instead the street ended in a narrow alley, and alley led to yet another alley.

This was definitely not the right direction.

Nic chewed the inside of her lip. The sun had dropped, but the heat was still intense, and there were fewer people out now.

Nic batted a fly buzzing her face and sighed. She couldn't panic. She hadn't been gone that long. Twenty minutes. Thirty at the most.

She rubbed the back of her arm across her eyes, catching the dampness on her brow. Think. Which way did you come? Where was the sun? In Baraka the markets—like the mosques—are built facing East. All she had to do was orient herself to the East and she'd find her way across.

Malik was waiting at the side of the car when Fatima arrived alone. "Is the princess here?" Fatima asked, bending down to peer into the darkened car windows.

He felt as if his heart stopped, his muscles turned to stone. "She's supposed to be with you."

Fatima looked at him, wide-eyed, innocent. "I thought we were together. We were just browsing through the market—"

"You lost her."

"No."

"*You* lost her."

His normally quiet voice boomed. Fatima shook her head. "I didn't. I thought she was with me. I was sure she was following me."

He snapped his fingers, and his driver appeared. "The princess is missing." He spoke quickly, urgently. "Summon the security officers, let them know we must find her. In the meantime, I'm going to call the palace, request additional guard.''

The chauffeur bowed, hurried away. Fatima watched Malik call the palace on his phone, tears in her eyes. ''I didn't mean to lose her, cousin. I wouldn't do that.''

He silenced her with a lift of his hand. ''I don't want to hear it. You've had a problem with the princess since she arrived.'' He turned his back on her, spoke to the captain of his military guard, requesting assistance, giving the captain his location at the market square.

Tears continued to well in Fatima's eyes. ''Forgive me, cousin.''

But he couldn't look at her. ''I trusted you,'' he said, his deep voice curt, his tone bitter. ''And you have shamed me.''

Fatima climbed into the back of the limousine and buried her face in her hands. Malik paced before the car, waiting for the driver to return. Malik intended to set off and look for Nicolette himself, but suddenly she was there, a flushed princess, hot, tired, but obviously grateful to have found her way back. ''You're still here.'' Nic smiled in relief. ''Thank goodness.''

''I'd never leave you.''

''I know, but I—''

''I'd never leave you.'' His gaze swept her, a quick inspection to ensure she was truly in one piece. ''Are you okay?''

''I'm fine. Just embarrassed. I don't know how I managed to lose Fatima.'' Nic paused, glanced around. ''Is she back yet?''

Malik's expression darkened. ''She's in the car.''

''Good. I was afraid she was out looking for me, and I didn't want to put her in any danger.'' Nic shook her head, incredulous. ''It's hot.''

''It is,'' he agreed, spotting the driver returning through the square with the security officers. ''Let me take care of this,'' he said, indicating the officers approaching, ''and then we'll head back to the palace.''

Back at the palace, Nic returned to her suite and discovered Alea waiting with open arms. ''Are you alright, Princess?'' Alea cried, touching Nic's arm as if she were an apparition.

Alea's concern was almost comical. ''I'm fine.'' Nic grimaced. ''I was lost. The city was hot. But I found my way back and everything's okay.''

''Well, we're going to take good care of you,'' Alea assured Nicolette. ''First, a shower to cool you off, wash away the dust, then a good soak in the hot tub, after that, a massage, help relax every muscle—''

''That's not necessary, Alea. A shower is all I need.''

But the young woman wasn't listening. She was already off, heading into Nicolette's luxurious bathroom, opening doors, turning on the shower. ''Come, Princess,'' Alea called above the steamy shower spray. ''Let's get you started.''

An hour and a half later, Nicolette winced as the experienced masseuse dug her elbows into the knots in Nicolette's back. The massage wasn't Swedish style, Nic thought, wincing again, but after an hour of steady kneading, rubbing, twisting, Nic was beginning to feel boneless.

But gradually the deep tissue massage gave way to a softer touch, longer strokes that soothed instead of hurt. Relaxed beyond belief, Nic drifted in and out of sleep, happy to just lie there and be mindless.

No worries now, she thought sleepily. It'd be impossible to worry.

The masseuse finished by working Nic's hands, feet, lightly kneading, working each little joint.

Stepping from the table the masseuse held up Nic's warm silk robe. ''Your Highness.''

Nic dragged herself off the massage table, her limbs so heavy, she wanted to slide into bed. Instead she forced her arms into the robe's quilted sleeves and belted the tie around her waist. ''Thank you.''

''My pleasure.'' The masseuse opened the door, gestured to Nic's pink marble bathroom. ''The steam room, Your Highness?''

''No thank you, not again. I think I'll just shower.''

''As you wish.'' The masseuse bowed, and excused herself and Alea appeared.

''How do you feel, Princess?''

''Lovely.'' Nic covered her mouth, hiding her yawn. ''I can't even keep my eyes open.''

''You won't have to. Rinse off the oil and then I'll finish you off with a nice scented lotion to keep your skin soft. Afterward, you can put your robe back on and you'll find refreshments waiting for you in your sitting room.''

Nicolette spent forever in the shower, letting the hot water rain down on her head. She couldn't remember when she last felt so languid. She was relaxed, almost too relaxed, she didn't feel the slightest urgency...about anything. She shampooed her hair, once, twice, and then finished with the delicious fruit scented conditioner that made Nic's mouth water.

After finally stepping from the shower and toweling dry, Nic allowed Alea to slather her in lotion. She couldn't protest the indulgence even if she wanted to. She simply didn't have the energy. The heat from the market place, and then the two hours of pampering, had taken all speech away. Nic might as well have been a rag doll.

With her hair lightly blowed dry, Nic slipped on a clean robe, this one a gorgeous coral silk embroidered with gold and green threads, and headed for the sitting room where hot mint tea and sweets waited.

But that wasn't all that waited.

Malik Nuri waited as well.

Nic froze in the doorway, one hand going to her chest, checking the drape and coverage of her thin silk robe. ''Your Highness.''

''I thought I'd join you for tea.''

She'd never felt self-conscious around any man before and yet Malik did something to her, made her feel absolutely naked. And truthfully, right now she was rather naked. Her silk robe didn't conceal much.

''It is your palace,'' she said, tension curling in the pit of her stomach.

His eyebrow lifted. ''That's not the same thing as a 'yes, I'm glad to see you', is it?''

Nic licked her bottom lip, conscious she wore absolutely nothing beneath the robe, not a chemise or even a thong. Just skin. Warm, still slightly damp skin from her hot shower and application of body lotion.

And he knew it, she thought, with a curiously expectant shiver.

''Of course I'd enjoy your company,'' she said, surprised yet again by her flutter of nerves. She shouldn't have this kind of response—at the very least, she shouldn't act on this response.

"Any company?" he teased. "Not my company?"

Her gaze took in the way he reclined on the sofa cushions, his own robe open at the chest, his long muscular legs covering the length of the settee.

He was gorgeous. And he knew it. "You know I enjoy your company," she answered softly.

"And my touch."

She had to bite the inside of her cheek to keep from laughing. "Did it ever cross your mind that you're still single because you're arrogant and conceited?"

He smiled. "I'm not conceited."

"But arrogant?"

"*Laeela*, I wouldn't be a proper sultan if I didn't have a certain amount of confidence."

CHAPTER EIGHT

His smile was slow, wicked, and rising from the couch Malik walked to a console panel on one of the walls. He touched a few buttons, and music sounded, spilling from hidden speakers. It wasn't Eastern music, but a popular rock and roll ballad. "You did say the other night you wanted to dance."

She couldn't tear her gaze from the small smile playing at his lips. He was tall, dark, handsome in a bone-melting kind of way. "I didn't think you danced with women."

"Not in public."

She couldn't speak, adrenaline coursing through her veins and he moved toward her, his energy leashed, his powerful body graceful, languid. "But then," he added in that deep sexy voice of his, "there's lots of things I can't do in public that I love to do in private."

He stood before her, arms loose at his sides, his chest bare. "Come here."

Her mouth had grown dry and Nic shook her head in a desperate plea for sanity. "You have no dinner engagements tonight?"

"None."

She touched the tip of her tongue to her lips, trying to moisten them. "No appointments?"

"Completely free." His smile was in his eyes. His arms were strong, relaxed. He had all night. He could afford to wait. "I thought you'd like this song."

The group was one of her favorite bands. She'd met the band members on their last European tour, too. "I do."

"So come here."

She didn't know why she couldn't go to him, but her legs wouldn't move, her feet felt rooted to the floor, and dread hummed through her, reminding her that she was not who or what she seemed. "You come to me," she whispered, praying he wouldn't, praying he'd turn and walk away.

He laughed. He was so confident he could find her insolence amusing. Malik closed the distance between them, pulled her against him, shaping her body to his, silver gaze glinting with laughter. "Like this, princess?"

She shuddered at the press of his thighs, his body hard, his torso firm. Nic's eyes closed as Malik bent his head, pulled back her robe and kissed her bare shoulder.

He must have felt her shudder as he kissed the same sensitive spot again and this time as the shiver raced through her, he cupped the side of her breast, feeling her nipple harden in his hand.

Her legs went weak and she hid her face against his chest as the music wound around them, warm, seductive, intimate. Nic found herself drawn closer against Malik's chest, his smooth hard bicep pressed to her shoulder. She liked his arms around her. She liked the way he slid his hands down her ribcage, as if counting each rib, shaping each rib, until he reached her hip bones. He knew how to make a woman feel like a woman, and when he rested his hands in the small of her spine, she thought she could stay that way forever, savoring his warm, his spicy fragrance, how easy he was with her. No strangeness, no awkwardness. No formality. No royal games.

Just Malik and Nic.

She felt a twinge of guilt. Make that Malik and Chantal. But she didn't want to be Chantal anymore. She wanted to be herself with him. She wanted him to want *Nic*.

Impulsively she reached up and touched his prominent cheekbone, tracing the sweeping length of bone and the shape of his chin. Everything in his face was strong, everything in his eyes was mysterious. Yet she knew he'd answer any question she put to him. He'd talk openly, candidly, about any subject she chose.

What would it be like to love you? She silently wondered, letting her hand return to his shoulder, feeling emotion grow and swell inside her chest, her heart strangely tender. For a second her eyes burned, little pricks of pain everywhere.

She'd love to spend hours with him. She'd love to take it all so slow. No rush, no hurry, no goal. Just time together.

She'd never been one of those glassy-eyed optimistics. She

didn't believe in excess of hope, didn't believe in romantic dreams that couldn't be fulfilled. Dreaming for her was a precursor to action. If she desired it, she did it. It wasn't a challenge but a fact. If there was something she wanted out of life, she went for it.

"Thinking about Lilly?" Malik asked, interrupting her thoughts, his fingers playing her spine, sending rivulets of feeling in every direction.

Nic shook her head, feeling guilty. He must think she was a terrible mother. She sighed heavily. She was in this so deep, wasn't she?

What was she doing here? What was happening between them? They were on a collision course with disaster.

Nic felt as if she were beginning to suffocate and she stepped back, putting space between them so she could try to think. "Can we sit down?"

"Certainly." He took a seat, and she knew he expected her to join him, but she hesitated. If she sat next to him in her little flimsy robe she might as well give up the battle now. If he touched her again, peeled the robe from her shoulders, kissed that sensitive spot on her neck, or her collarbone, she'd hold his lips to her skin and ask him to just keep on going...

"Maybe I should go put some clothes on first."

"Why?"

"You know why."

He cocked his head, studying her. "I can't believe you're so afraid to make love with me."

Talk about honesty. Nicolette flushed. "If you were a terrible kisser we wouldn't have a problem."

He rubbed his brow, ruffling his crisp black hair. "I could try to kiss badly. If that's what would make you happy."

She groaned, exasperated. "It wouldn't."

"You're very difficult to please, Princess."

"Yes. I know." Nic felt like she was losing her mind. "Even more so than usual."

"What's wrong?"

She pressed her hands to her head, trying to quiet all the guilty recriminations, the little voices that wouldn't let her rest. "I think I'm developing a split-personality."

Malik had to work very hard at keeping a straight face. ''Really?''

''Yes.''

''Tell me about them.''

Nic paced in front of him. ''There's the virtuous Chantal,'' she said, shooting him a swift glance, ''and then there's the impulsive Chantal, the one that really likes you.''

''So what is the problem?''

She stopped pacing. ''If I don't even know who the real me is, how will you?''

''I can tell.'' He gestured to her. ''Come here.''

He was making her nerves dance, and she moved toward him, drawn to him despite her better judgment.

Malik reached up to clasp her hand, his fingers locking with hers, and smoothly, firmly, he drew her down onto his lap, and she gasped at the naked touch of skin. Her thighs rested against his, and even though they were wearing their robes, the silk fabric didn't contain him. He was aroused and his body pressed against her, teasing her tender flesh, making her even more sensitive.

His hands curved around her hips, his fingers firm on her hipbones and he tilted her hips forward, and back, shifting her pelvis between his large strong hands.

''You belong to me.'' He placed a kiss on her mouth. ''Married or unmarried, queen or friend, you can call us what you want, but you,'' and he shifted her again, pulling her forward so his erection rubbed inside her thighs, at the apex of her thighs, ''you were made for me, and I for you.''

Her mouth had gone dry. She couldn't think of a single thing to say. Of course she wasn't his, and there was no way she belonged to him, but it'd been years since she felt this raw physical craving for anyone.

''Do you do this with all your wives?'' she asked breathlessly.

''Harems are passé,'' he answered, his hand rising to cup her breast through the silk fabric, his thumb strumming her nipple, playing the taut peak as if he had all the time in the world. And indeed, he did. He was planning on keeping her, making her his wife legally, and in Baraka wives were permanent.

Oh, if he kept touching her like that, she'd do just about anything. She linked her hands around his shoulders, needing to hang tight and as he strummed her nipple his other hand played on her hip.

Nic couldn't stand the tension within her. She dragged herself closer to him. "I want you." Her voice sounded faint, breathless, and indeed, she was seeing stars, her vision dark and silvery all at the same time.

"I know," he said, and he kept playing her body, playing the nerves and she was shivering against him, dancing a helpless dance.

She felt heat rush through her in a torrential wave. He'd turned her so on, turned her into an inferno. She felt her skin prickle and burn across her cheekbones, along her brow and even her lips felt hot, full, aching.

"No, Malik, you don't know how much I want you. You just think you do…" She bent her head, pressed her face to his neck, breathed in his spicy cologne and the warm scent that was him, and he smelled delicious, smelled like everything she wanted in life.

Keep me, a tiny voice whispered inside her. Keep me forever and never let me go. It'd been since Daniel, she thought, reaching for Malik again, sliding her hands up through his hair, tightening her fingers against his scalp, feeling the crisp cool strands of Malik's hair bunch in her fist.

"I think I know what you need," he whispered against her mouth, pulling her closer so that their two bodies felt almost as one.

And as close as they were, it still wasn't enough. Nic needed to be possessed by, filled by him. There'd been years of dates and several lovers since Daniel but no one made her feel like this anymore, no one made her want like this. This was as hot and intense as she'd ever known. "Can we make love? Is it illegal to be intimate before the wedding?"

"It's not illegal." His lips brushed the corner of her mouth. "If it were, I'd change the law." He lifted her long heavy hair from her neck, stroked her sensitive nape.

She shuddered against him. He held her in his thrall. He was powerful but he never used force. He didn't need to speak harshly, or use strong language. He didn't need threats or boasts. He wore his confidence like his silken robe. Comfortably.

Naturally. He'd do anything for his people. He'd protect them at all costs. He'd protect her, too.

Malik lay her down on the settee, and stretched out over her, his weight braced on his elbows. "You're trapped," he said, studying her lying beneath him. "My prisoner."

"So what are you going to do to me?"

His gaze settled on her mouth. "Make you talk."

"Talk?"

"I want to know what you think about when you go so quiet on me." He traced her lips with the tip of his finger, lightly following the bow shaped curve of the upper lip and the swollen lower lip. "I want to know what you don't talk about."

She felt her lips quiver from his caress. "Why do we always have to talk?"

"Because I want to make sure you know what you're doing. I want to make sure I know what you're thinking. Better to face the facts than run away from them."

He was caressing her ear, lightly running his fingertip along the curve of her outer ear and then gently along the sensitive lobe.

She couldn't think when he was doing that, couldn't concentrate on anything but the way he made her body blister and burn. "All right. Ask me a question."

"What does no one know about you?"

What did no one know about her?

She tried to blot out the delicious sensations he was stirring within her, by staring up at the elegant domed ceiling, all gold and cobalt-blue tiles, and the breeze outside the open window rustled the thick date leaves. What did no one know about her? What had she kept hidden from everyone for all these years?

Daniel, of course.

She'd fallen for him so hard.

He'd worked at the palace. A mechanical engineer. Daniel built and restored race cars and she'd wanted it to work between them, had wanted to be with him as much as she could, but their relationship was doomed from the start. Perhaps her father could get away with marrying her mother, but there was no way she could run off with Daniel Thierry. No way she could live with him. No way she could love him. But that didn't stop her from wanting him with a desperation that nearly drove her mad.

She might have run off with him too, if it hadn't been for Chantal's wedding to Prince Armand. Somehow Nic couldn't run away with Daniel when Chantal was marrying a man she didn't love in hopes of protecting Melio's future.

Chantal had been such a beautiful bride—not radiant the way magazines liked to say—but poised, ethereal in her loveliness. With her warm brown hair and gray eyes she looked like a Dresden figurine. Perfect. Flawless. Petite. Her full skirts and long veil with the high diamond tiara captured the fairy tale elements of the royal wedding and her picture was on the front of nearly two hundred magazines the week after the wedding.

Chantal was happy, Nic assured herself, not blissful, but happy enough.

Yet the fact that Chantal had the strength and conviction to go through with an arranged marriage undermined Nic's insistence on doing only what she pleased.

Truth was, she couldn't run away with her beautiful Daniel.

Truth was, there couldn't be a future with Daniel.

He might kiss her senseless, and he might make her laugh, and she might feel most comfortable with him, but he wasn't even remotely what Melio needed.

A month after Chantal's lavish wedding Nicolette ended it with Daniel.

It was the hardest thing she'd ever done as an adult. In fact, she changed her mind once, getting back together with him for a stolen night, but later, the next day, she forced herself to call him and make a complete break.

He was out shopping when he answered his phone. She could hear the voices of other shoppers, could hear him periodically place things in his basket, could hear the mundane sounds of normal life all around him and it cut her, realizing in that moment it was really all over. She'd never be part of his real world again. She'd never do the ordinary things with him that she'd wanted to do. No trips to the movies, no snuggling under the covers late on Sunday morning, no going out on the spur of the moment for sushi or Chinese.

Don't take my calls, she'd said. Don't let me change my mind.

In the store, in the middle of his shopping, Daniel went quiet. He'd said absolutely nothing.

She'd felt the tears rise, felt the distance growing by the second. No one had made her feel so good about herself, and losing him—leaving him, was breaking her heart.

She had to talk quickly to get the rest of the words out, and they came in a rush. "If you see my number, don't pick up," she said, holding the tears back. "If I show up at the garage, don't talk to me. Don't let me change my mind."

"If that's what you want," he finally said.

Is that what she wanted? No. Is that what Melio needed? Yes. She held the phone tighter, closed her eyes, and tried to be responsible. Think about Grandmama and Grandfather, she told herself. Think about Joelle. Think about all the people who have worked and sacrificed to get us to this point.

"It's what's right," she said, emotion strangled inside of her, strangling her. If only he'd give her a good reason to throw respectability and responsibility away.

But he didn't. He'd been a citizen of Melio his whole life. Yes, he'd gone to school in Rome, studied beneath the great DeLaurent family, but when he'd come into his own, he'd returned to his island kingdom and like everyone else, he understood the burden on the Ducasses, knew that one day the princesses would inherit.

He'd known from the beginning their relationship could go nowhere. But he'd taken a chance. Gone with his heart. And she had to admire that. The odds hadn't been good, but Daniel had let the love carry him as far it would, and when it ended, he'd been a man.

He'd let her go without a word of complaint.

Staring up at the gold and blue domed ceiling, Nicolette blinked back tears. Giving up Daniel had put her emotions into a deep, cold storage and for the first time in a long time she could admit what her decision had cost her.

True love. A chance at lasting happiness.

She felt Malik's gaze. He'd been patiently waiting for her answer. "I've no secrets," she said at last. "My life is public knowledge."

He leaned forward, took her chin in his hand, turning her head to stare into her eyes. "Yet you cry."

She tensed. "I'm not crying."

"I see tears. And sadness. You lost something and it's never been returned."

My heart, she agreed silently, even as she masked her surprise that he'd read her so accurately, that he'd nailed the emotion and need. "My parents died when I was ten."

"This isn't about your parents—"

He was interrupted by a rapid knock on the door. The outer door opened and Alea's young voice could be heard calling for admittance. "Your Highness, forgive the interruption, but you're needed immediately."

Malik sat up, closed his robe. "What's happened?"

"Lady Fatima, Your Highness. They've called an ambulance for her. She's terribly ill."

Nic waited for Malik to return. He did not. Instead he had servants bring Nicolette a dinner tray to her room.

Later a grim-faced Alea appeared to help Nicolette prepare for bed. Alea didn't volunteer any information about Fatima, and out of politeness, Nic didn't ask.

But once Alea left, carrying away the remnants of dinner, Nicolette paced her room. She was concerned about Fatima despite how the other woman had treated her. And after what had been interrupted between herself and Malik she felt like she was going crazy. She wanted to make love, not fall in love. She wanted passion, not emotion. She wanted to be with Malik now, not committing to the future.

Why was this so hard? She'd been with other men before, had made love but hadn't worried about falling in love. Why couldn't she do that here? Why couldn't she stay breezy, light, keep it all superficial?

Because Malik wasn't superficial, that's why.

Nic slumped on the foot of her bed, pressed her fists to her eyes. She could see him even now, handsome, proud, intelligent, kind…

God, he was kind. He had such warmth and dignity and she couldn't bear to hurt him. Disappoint him.

But she was. No matter what she did now, it'd disappoint. No matter what choice, it'd be wrong.

He wanted Chantal. She was Nic. He wanted forever. She only believed in the moment.

She didn't even believe in marriage for heaven's sake!

Letting her hands fall to her sides, Nic inhaled slowly, trying to calm the wild beasts stampeding inside her. Breathe, she told herself, just breathe.

But it was a struggle to even breathe. It was such a struggle being here, pretending to be someone she wasn't. She'd stopped trying to pretend that she was handling the situation well.

What she needed to do was reduce it to the most elemental form, and in this case, it was physical attraction. Sexual attraction.

She wanted to make love with Malik. Maybe making love is just an escape, another form of running away, but at least making love, she'd feel something besides this…panic.

Making love she'd feel like herself again.

She hated pretending to be Chantal. She missed her natural hair color, missed her own strengths, and missed her own dreams.

If she could just become Nic again. If she could just find her sense of humor, and sense of adventure, again.

If she could just stop worrying about Melio, her grandparents, Chantal and Lilly, and the kind of future Joelle faced as well.

Her brow creased as she stared across her room to the door with the delicate arch. It was a lot to worry about.

But if she could just escape the worries for a while…

If she could just be with Malik, feel his arms around her, put her cheek on his chest…

If she could just close her eyes and think about nothing but sharing the moment with him. Just be close to him. Warm skin, his body, his heart beating beneath her ear…

And maybe his hands taking hers, pinning her arms down against the bed, his mouth on hers, his body moving over…

Maybe his body in hers…

Maybe…

Nic bit her knuckle, feeling as if she were dangerously close to losing control. She—who'd needed so few people in her life—had never felt as if she needed anyone or anything like one long intense night in Malik's bed. He was a king. He had to know what she was feeling. He carried so many responsibilities on his shoulders. Surely he could give her some advice.

Or at least, be able to help her forget.

Just to be a person. A woman. Just to be Nicolette and·loved for herself, wanted for herself…

Nic fell asleep waiting for some word from Malik and early the next morning, woke with an even heavier heart than before.

She had to go. That's all there was to it. Time to go home, wash out this awful brown hair color, answer her mail, check her email, start dating again…

She swallowed hard, hating the lump that filled her throat. She'd miss Malik. She liked looking at him, liked listening to him, just liked him period.

Nic showered, dressed, wondered where breakfast was. Leaving her room she noticed a small congregation of servants in the hall. The gathering of servants troubled her. She hung back in the shadows watching the servants speak. She knew enough of palace life to know that the small groups of guards and servants meeting, murmuring, parting, only to assemble again further down the hall was not normal palace protocol.

Something was definitely wrong, and from the hushed tones of the guards and servants the problem had to be serious.

Had Fatima been sick before, and Nic didn't know?

Guilt assailed Nicolette. What if Fatima had been recovering from something…in remission from cancer or leukemia?

Nicolette returned to her room, quietly shut the door, worrying about Fatima without really knowing what Fatima was facing.

Alea arrived a little later with coffee and a message from the sultan. Nicolette opened the folded sheet of paper. He'd written a note, letting her know that due to Fatima's poor health, the morning's language lesson had been cancelled.

CHAPTER NINE

MALIK sat in a chair next to Fatima's bed, his hands folded together, his expression grim. His thoughts raced, confusion and anger. "I don't understand."

Fatima's dark head turned away. "I can't talk about it."

"You have to," he shot back, his deep voice curt, tense. How could she do this? What on earth had she been thinking?

Fatima wouldn't answer. She continued staring at the wall and Malik felt a welling of helpless rage. He rose from the chair, towered over the bed. "They wanted to keep you overnight at the hospital. Maybe I was wrong to bring you home. Maybe I should take you back—"

"No." She rolled over, looked up at him, tears in her eyes. "I won't do it again."

She looked so small, so defenseless and his anger melted. He loved Fatima like a sister. They'd grown up together. He trusted her. "But why would you try something like that in the first place? What if help hadn't come in time?" He shook his head, exhausted, worn out from the night spent at the side of her bed. "Is your life really so unbearable?"

She covered her face with her hands, unable to bear his censure. "Forgive me."

"Help me understand."

She cried harder. Malik felt sick at heart. "I've sent for your mother," he said after a long moment. "She and your sister are coming from New York."

"No, Malik!" She scrubbed her face dry, struggled to sit up, grimacing at a wave of nausea. They'd pumped her stomach at the hospital and she was obviously still sore. "Mother will be furious. She'll be so upset."

"And I'm not?" he demanded, not knowing whether to shake her or put his arms around her. "Fatima, you could have died."

She shuddered. "It was a mistake. I knew it was a mistake the moment I did it. That's why I called for help."

"But why?" He couldn't let it drop. He couldn't let it go. You didn't swallow a bottle of pills without good reason. What had pushed her over the edge? "Fatima, you must be honest with me. I insist."

She looked at him, then past him, her dark gaze going vacant. "You were supposed to marry me."

He froze, air bottled in his lungs. *What?*

Staring down into Fatima's averted face, he could see her agony. Her face was still pale, her mouth pinched, her eyes glassy, and he felt her tremor of fear and anger, hurt and confusion. Her agony was real. "Explain this to me," he said more gently, trying for a calm he didn't feel.

She wouldn't meet his gaze. "Father said you were to be my husband. He said I was to wait for you."

His heart fell.

For a long moment he felt horribly destructive—look what he'd done to Fatima? And then reason set in. He hadn't done anything to her but treat her as a member of his own family.

And now he wracked his brain, trying to think of a time when marriage with Fatima might have been discussed, but he could remember no such conversation. It was common practice in Baraka for cousins to marry, for family to intermarry. Cousins were considered favorable marriage partners as it consolidated a family's power.

Fatima filled the silence with her slow, painful words. "It'd been widely assumed that we would marry—"

"By whom?"

"My family. Your family."

"I've never heard this before."

She shrugged wearily. "My father said your father had agreed. It would keep the wealth in the family, simplify inheritance." Her body slumped, no energy left. "Ever since I was small, I'd been raised to think that you…and I…" Her voice drifted away, she bit her lip, trying to hold back the tears.

You and I rang in his head. You and I… "So you took an overdose of sleeping pills?"

She shrugged yet again, her slender spine bent beneath the weight of it all. "I didn't understand why you'd decided to go elsewhere for your bride when you have me here single, waiting.''

And suddenly he understood. Not just her pain, but also her shame.

In the West, Fatima was still considered young; she was just in her mid-twenties, but in Baraka that was old for women who remained unmarried. Men didn't believe a woman couldn't remain pure—untouched—for that many years and a bride's purity was as important as her dowry. Indeed, a great part of the wedding celebration was the confirmation of the bride's virginity.

Malik sat down in the chair next to her bed, reached for her hands, held them between his own. She felt so cold, her skin chilled. "I didn't realize—" He broke off, heartsick. Or did he?

He'd known she'd always hoped to make a royal marriage. But he hadn't realized she'd always hoped to marry him...or had he?

He clasped her cold hands in his, trying to warm her. His thoughts were broken, disjointed. He'd confronted her this morning wanting to make sure she understood the shame she'd brought on the family by her actions, and yet now he saw the shame she'd been enduring for years.

People would have been wondering, whispering, why a wealthy royal like Fatima Nuri was still single. They would have wondered why her cousin went outside Baraka for a wife...they would have gossiped about Fatima's reputation, and her shame. Shame. *Hshuma*, he thought wearily. *Hshuma* was such a heavy burden for everyone.

She bowed her head, stared at her hands. "Forgive me."

"I do." He felt her tremble and his heart smote him. He'd unwittingly hurt her. No wonder Fatima had been so angry, so resentful of Nicolette. Fatima had feel rejected. Supplanted.

Fatima couldn't bring herself to meet his eyes. "What have you told my family?"

Nothing yet, thank God. "Just that you were very ill, and they needed to come quickly."

"Ah." Fatima gently disengaged her hands, putting distance between them. "When do they arrive?"

"Later today."

"Will you tell Mother about what I...did?"

He'd been asking himself the same thing. What did one do

in this circumstance? "No," he decided quickly, and knew it was the right decision. There was absolutely no reason to bring more shame to her, or on the family. "But you have to know this behavior—what you did—isn't acceptable. The choice you made, that's not a valid option. You are loved by all. Your life is of great value—"

"Please," she pleaded, fresh tears welling. "Please don't. I won't do it again, I won't try anything like that again. I just felt so ashamed, so horrible about what happened at the market yesterday. I'd never mean to hurt the princess and yet—" She broke off, shook her head, tears spilling. "Maybe I did lose her on purpose. I don't know anymore—"

He hugged her. That any member of his family should hurt so hurt him. "The princess returned safe. Do not worry, or blame yourself anymore. You must get rest. You need to take care of yourself."

She nodded slowly, fatigue etched in the tightness at her eyes and mouth. "Maybe I'll go with Mother to New York for awhile. Maybe a change of pace…"

"I'll arrange it for you." Malik kissed her forehead, and stood. "You've nothing to worry about, Fatima. Just get some rest. Everything will work out."

"Malik." Her voice stopped him at the door. He turned around to face her. Fatima's eyes looked huge in her pale face. "I…can I ask a favor, please?"

He nodded.

"Would you consider taking the princess to Zefd for a few days…just while Mother is here? It'd be easier to pack and leave for NY without worrying about Mother saying something to Princess Chantal. I know Mother will be disappointed that I didn't—" She broke off, frowned, drew a deep breath. "You see, Mother had also hoped you and I…and she doesn't know about your engagement to Princess Chantal."

He nodded. "I understand. I'd planned on taking the princess there next week, we'll just go a few days early. You're comfortable explaining my absence to your mother?"

Fatima smiled weakly. "Yes. And thank you, cousin."

Malik stopped by Nicolette's room personally to tell her they were going to visit another home of his for a few days. Nicolette saw the shadows in his eyes, felt his strain. "How is Fatima?"

He shook his head.

His silence put knots in her stomach. "If she's ill, we shouldn't go—"

"She'll be herself soon. I don't want you to worry. You have enough on your mind."

"But—"

"No." This time he was adamant, his tone forceful. "I do not want to discuss this further. Have Alea pack. Tell her you are going to Zefd."

Several hours later Nicolette and Malik left noisy, congested Atiq behind, traveling in a luxuriously outfitted four wheel drive vehicle, the interior seats leather, the windows tinted, the middle console between two of the passenger seats built to house a mini refrigerator, a stereo, and a DVD player.

Malik sat silent the first half hour of the trip, staring blindly out the window. Nicolette knew he wasn't angry with her. Rather he was wrestling internally, in a battle with himself.

Finally she wouldn't let him sit in silence any longer. He'd had over an hour to beat himself up. Now he'd have to talk to her.

"I've never seen a four-wheel drive vehicle like this," she said, her voice breaking the heavy silence.

"It's custom," he answered, his expression even more brooding. "Built for the desert. To handle the dunes if necessary."

"It's quite plush. You could live in here."

"If necessary."

He wasn't making this easy, but Nicolette doggedly inspected the entertainment system, remembering the hidden speakers and stereo system in her room at the palace. "Lots of interesting gadgets."

"A king should be entitled to a few play things."

She cocked her head, hearing the anger and self-loathing in his voice. What had happened last night? What had happened with his cousin? "Please tell me about Fatima."

"There's nothing to say."

Pain deepened his voice and Nic's heart ached. "I've been worried," she said softly. "And I know you care about her very much."

Malik continued to stare out the windows. The hills were giving way to steep red tinted mountains. "She's going to go to

New York for a while, spend time with her family there. She agrees with me that she needs a change—''

"And until then, we're leaving her alone?"

"She won't be alone. Her mother and sister are arriving from America this afternoon."

Nic assessed the situation, understanding suddenly that she was being sent away deliberately before Fatima's mother arrived. "You didn't want me to meet your aunt."

"Fatima wanted to avoid any potential problems."

"Meeting your aunt would have created problems?"

He turned his head, met her gaze. "My aunt wished me to marry my cousin, and Fatima, wisely wanted to save you, and herself, from further embarrassment."

So that explained Fatima's hostility. Nic exhaled slowly, thinking of the past week, all the time the two had been forced to spend together. Fatima must have felt hurt, and humiliated. "I didn't know."

He made a rough sound, impatient, angry. "I didn't, either."

Her lips parted in surprise but Malik's pained expression stilled the words on her lips, leaving them unspoken. He looked staggered even now. Nicolette had never seen him so quiet, so closed. It was as if he'd gone inward and shut all his emotions down.

Something horrible must have happened last night… "I'm sorry, Malik. I really am."

"I am, too."

Nicolette suddenly wondered if perhaps she'd done something far worse by coming here than just masquerading as Chantal. Had she perhaps destroyed people's futures…their lives? "Was there a reason you couldn't marry?"

His powerful shoulders shifted. "I didn't choose her," he said flatly, turning to look at Nicolette with a piercing gaze. He stared at her hard, staring at her as if he could see all the way through her. "I chose you."

Nicolette felt a wave of panic. Fatima loved Malik, she'd hoped to share her life with him, and all the while Nicolette was playing a part, biding her time before she could escape back to Melio.

How would Nic's disappearance affect Malik…Fatima…the Nuri family?

She swayed on her seat, feeling dizzy, sick, scared of what she'd started. Her breezy words spoken to Chantal returned to haunt her, I'll sneak in, sneak out, and be gone before the sultan even notices...

Wrong.

"She's going to be okay," Malik said, sensing Nicolette's panic, seeking to reassure her. "Don't blame yourself. I chose you. You didn't create this...problem."

Nicolette heard the emotion in Malik's voice, felt his worry, his personal struggle. He blamed himself.

He cared about Fatima. He loved his family. He'd spent his life trying to protect those he cared about. And in that instant, Nic realized that all those European gossip magazines had gotten King Malik Roman Nuri wrong. He wasn't a Casanova. It'd be impossible for him to take women to bed just to discard them later.

Malik cared about women. He didn't take advantage of them.

She felt tears start to her eyes. "No wonder you enjoy your gadgets." She covered his hand with hers. "You should be entitled to a few fun toys. It's not easy being King."

He lifted her hand to his mouth, kissed the back of her fingers. He was trying hard to lighten his mood. "You will enjoy Zefd. It will be good for us to spend a few days in the mountains."

But Nic didn't want him to put on a happy face for her sake. She searched his eyes. "Are you going to be okay?"

Leaning forward, he brushed his mouth across her cheek, and then once more on her lips. "I'm glad you're with me, *laeela.*"

"I'm glad I'm here, too."

They spent two hours traveling in and out of the rugged red and pink mountains, climbing slowly, steadily to the peak of one mountain, to descend on the other side, and then start climbing all over again.

Late afternoon they reached an open valley, the barren ground dotted here and there with oases of green. "Artificial lakes," Malik said, "for commercial orchards of date trees."

On this side of the mountains the landscape looked brighter, clearer, and more unusual. It was the quality of light, Nic thought, the way the golden rays hit the rose and gold sand, reflecting off the pink and red granite cliffs.

Everything here seemed to come from the earth, to be made

of the earth, and would eventually return to the earth. The driver approached a red sandstone fortress, the stark walls high, the parapet clearly etched against the brilliant blue sky. The fortress towered over the rest of the city and yet was still dwarfed by the snow-capped mountains behind.

"So where are we?" Nic's inquisitive gaze took in the magnificent mountains dusted in white and the weathered apricot and terracotta buildings before them.

"This is Zefd. One of the oldest cities in Baraka. My father's family came from here."

As Malik's vehicle entered the walls of the city, people unexpectedly poured out, robed men and women and dozens of eager children. "Did they know you were coming?"

Malik's expression was ironic. "Someone must have alerted them."

The driver parked, but before he opened the door for them, palace guards appeared, forming a protective barrier between the sultan's car and the crowd.

Malik climbed from the car and assisted Nicolette. On seeing the king, the people cheered, and Malik lifted a hand in acknowledgment.

Malik was surprised when Nicolette moved forward, toward the crowd, greeting his people. She spoke only a few Arabic words, but the sincere phrases coupled with her warm smiles appeared to charm everyone.

Standing at her side, Malik watched Nicolette work the crowd, and while "work" sounded cold, it was exactly what she was doing. She knew her job, he thought, seeing how gracefully she handled the press of people, the hands extended, the small children lifted for her to kiss. She knew how long to chat, how long to listen, and then how to gently break free to continue making her way along the edge of the crowd.

He'd known she was strong, intelligent, but he hadn't expected this natural warmth and ease with his people. She was a true princess—regal, royal—and yet she identified with the common man. She would be good for his people.

And very good for him.

But he still hadn't made much headway when it came to knowing her, openly speaking with her. She'd learned to hide herself quite well. She projected so much warmth and charm that one didn't realize how neatly she sidestepped the personal until later.

Princess Nicolette did not wear her heart on her sleeve. Instead she kept her heart buried very deep. But it was her heart he wanted, and right now he wasn't even sure he had that. She was attracted to him, and responded to him, but the fact that she continued to hide her true identity had begun to trouble him. What if she didn't intend to go through with the wedding? What if she still intended to leave him at the altar, the jilted royal bridegroom?

The thought left him cold. His jaw gritted and he felt ice lodge in his chest, close to his heart. He wanted her. He needed her. He had no intention of losing her now.

His temper and emotions firmly in control, Malik moved forward, claimed Nicolette, drawing her with him into his desert home.

"We call this house the Citadel," he said, showing Nicolette around his Zefd desert home. "It was built as a fortress, and although the royal family has lived here off and on for the past two hundred years, it still serves as an important military outpost, one of our stronger defensive positions."

"Does Baraka worry about its neighbors?"

"The neighbors aren't the threat. Our troubles historically have come from within." He opened a door, leading to a large walled garden dominated by an ancient argan tree. The tree's upper limbs were enormous and gnarled, like spiny green dragons fighting.

They took a seat in the shade and were immediately served with glasses of ice cold, very sweet mint tea.

Malik's expression became contemplative and he drummed his fingers on the table. When he spoke next, he chose his words with care. "We have a complex society in Baraka, our culture that of Berber, Boudin, Arab, African. Throw in some French colonialism and you have intense conflicts."

She considered him. "How intense?"

"We've had more than our share of political turmoil in this century. Unfortunately, the last fifty years have been especially…explosive."

She reached for her glass, sipped the icy beverage gratefully. "The tensions have boiled over?"

"Violently."

"It seems I do need to learn Baraka's history," Nic said, setting her glass down.

He hesitated, staring off, his gaze on the red mountains beyond, the manicured palm trees lining the exterior citadel wall. "Baraka was in the midst of a violent civil war when I was born. This war lasted fifteen years. Everyone took sides. Many fought on behalf of the royal family, others fought for the insurgents. You see, we'd been under French rule for so long that people were fighting simply because they were angry, and scared, and no one knew what was best. I was still just a small child when my grandfather was assassinated, but I've never forgotten that day."

His brow furrowed as he remembered those dark violent years. "My grandfather's assassination ended the war." He turned and looked at her, his expression curiously blank. "Because you see, my grandfather was universally loved. He wasn't supposed to be killed. This wasn't a fight against him, or the family, but a fight about culture…custom…a fight to be recognized. The country virtually shut down the day of Grandfather's funeral. All the people took to the streets. I've never forgotten the sound of weeping, thousands of people weeping, and it taught me that nothing is more important than life. Than family."

"I'm surprised you haven't married before then."

"It didn't feel urgent."

"And it is now?"

His mouth opened as if to speak but instead he closed it, shook his head.

Truthfully, he'd never worried about marrying, having children, he'd been certain it was a matter of timing and sooner or later he'd meet the right woman…but it hadn't happened, and here he was, in his late thirties, and without a wife, an heir, or a family of his own.

And with one assassination attempt against him already.

Malik drank his tea, let the cool liquid pour down his throat and ice his raw emotions. It'd been a difficult twenty-four hour period. He was feeling the strain of Fatima's desperate measures, Nicolette's masquerade, and his own need for closure. He just wished he knew if she'd come through, meet him on her own terms. He wanted her on her terms, he wanted her heart, her laughter, her commitment. But he couldn't push her…yet.

He turned his head, looked at Nic whose features were grave, a deep furrow between her eyebrows from thinking hard, listening so intently.

"The years of war changed the way I looked at society," he continued. "It impacted the way I view our culture and the idea of stability. I learned early that we must embrace change, that without change we die."

"I would have thought you'd be afraid of change. After all, change triggered your grandfather's death—as well as that decade and half of turmoil. One would think you'd associate change with danger."

He shrugged. "But chaos and turmoil surround us, whether or not we choose to recognize it. Just because we don't see turmoil, or because we're not immediately impacted, doesn't negate its existence. Chaos can happen at any time."

"So your philosophy is…?"

Talking with Nic was good for him. "Change is good. Change is necessary. It doesn't mean that one can't revere the past and respect tradition, but tradition is pointless unless one can use tradition to teach, to use as a benchmark, to show one where and how to aim."

She leaned back in the chaise. "You like being King."

"I love being King."

CHAPTER TEN

NIC couldn't look away from his remarkable face with the light silver eyes. He was so quiet, so controlled. She'd had no idea he'd been through so much. Another man might have been angry, bitter, cruel, but Malik had accepted the tragedies with grace.

Baraka, she whispered to herself. *Baraka,* Fatima had once told her, meant Grace and peace. Malik had that peace, didn't he?

"There are dangers, of course," he said after a reflective silence, "but we all face danger at different points in our life. The secret is to be aware of the danger, to know how one is vulnerable, and then embrace truth, and life, and move on."

He rose, took her hand in his, and tugged her to her feet. "You still look hot, *laeela.* Let me take you to your room. You'll be pleased to know you have your own private swimming pool."

It was good news and Nic took a long, leisurely swim before dinner. The bottom and sides of the pool had been painted a sapphire blue and as Nic floated on her back, she stared up at the high pink stone towers surrounding her, one tower covered in purple bougainvillea, while climbing roses draped another tower wall, the petals the palest shade of pink. With jasmine and sweet orange blossoms scenting the air, and the setting sun painting the ancient walls a dusty red, Nicolette closed her eyes and felt…bliss. *Baraka,* she whispered to herself. Grace and peace.

Nicolette was to meet Malik in one of the walled courtyards for dinner. The Citadel staff had planned a special welcome supper for the princess, and the outdoor party delighted Nic, especially as it was a very exclusive party with just two guests—them.

A big bonfire had been built in the courtyard and a tent had been strung up to provide the sultan with additional privacy.

123

Malik had Nic sit beside him, cross-legged on a red woven rug, and together they dined on roasted lamb, artichokes, saffron rice, and endless nuts and sweets before sitting back to enjoy the evening's entertainment: a juggler—who juggled fire, talented singers, and traditional dancers.

The evening was unlike anything Nic had experienced in Atiq and was by far her favorite. She loved eating outside, relished the heat and glow of the fire, and embraced the sensuous beauty of the place. "If I was from Baraka, this is where I'd want to live," she said, resting her head on her knee, watching the flames crackle and dance. "This just feels right. I can't explain it, but it feels like...home."

Malik looked at her and a small muscle pulled in his jaw. "You say extraordinary things when I least expect it."

She turned her head from the fire, smiled at him. She felt pleasantly relaxed, a little bit sleepy. "What did I say?"

He gave his head a slight shake, drew an imaginary circle on the red blanket. "This is my home, my spiritual home. Whenever I have doubts, I come here."

"Doubts about what?"

His lips curved. "My ability to lead." His smile turned self-mocking. "As well as my struggle to find the balance between what I need, and what my people need."

Glancing at him, she saw that his brow had creased, and shadows haunted his eyes. He had such a noble face it hurt her to see him struggle. Nicolette felt her chest tighten. The depth of her emotion staggered her.

She wasn't supposed to care this much. She wasn't supposed to admire him. She wasn't supposed to want him.

She shouldn't have come to Zefd, shouldn't have loved the red mountains, the pinkish walls of the citadel, the gnarled trees that seemed to spring from the middle of the boulders. She shouldn't love the way the wind rustled the fronds on the date trees. Shouldn't like sitting on a carpet by a fire eating rice with her fingers and feeling peace, real peace, for the first time in years...

This *couldn't* happen. She couldn't fall in love with Malik or his desert or his kingdom. She wouldn't let herself want the conversations with him, the quiet with him, the life with him...

He was too soulful, too powerful. He'd turn her life upside

down. He'd expect her to give up everything she treasured, including her freedom and her beloved family at home.

Tears burned the back of her eyes. She felt as if she couldn't breathe properly. "I'm exhausted," she said, crossing her arms over her chest, overwhelmed by all that she felt sitting here in the dark with him. What she needed was time alone, quiet to figure out her way home. Melio felt light years away. How would she get back?

More importantly, how would she ever forget? If she left Malik, she'd leave her heart in Baraka with him.

"I'll walk you in," he said, rising.

"No need." Nic said hastily, trying to ignore the panic building inside of her. Whatever pretense she'd been able to manage had fallen behind like Atiq's white washed stonewalls. "You have dozens of valets and butlers and maids to escort me to bed."

"I know. I pay their salaries." He smiled sardonically. "But I am the sultan, and you, *laeela,* are my princess."

He walked her through the semidark corridors, candles lit in high wall sconces, the soft flickering yellow light reminding Nicolette of a medieval castle and yet the blue paint, and the gold and black mosaics were exotic instead of frightening.

He opened the door of her room, checked inside, made sure all was in order. "Is there anything you need?"

"No."

He said good night then, and left her. Nicolette shut the door, leaned against the door, wishing with all her might that Malik would have stayed. She needed to be with him. Needed to be close to him. Even if they never made love, she just wanted one night in his arms.

She slowly started to undress and a knock sounded on her door. Opening the door, Nic discovered Malik. A lump filled her throat. She was so glad to see him and it'd only been a couple minutes since he left. "Get lost?"

His crooked grin tugged on her heart. "I forgot something," he said.

"What?"

He wrapped his hands around her arms and pulled her against him. She felt the hard length of his body touch every soft curve of hers. Dropping his head, he kissed her. Malik's lips felt wonderfully cool against her heated skin and she closed her eyes.

"This," he murmured against her lips.

"You returned for a kiss?"

"What is more important than love?" With the tip of his finger he outlined her brow bone and then her small, straight nose.

She shivered at the touch, and yet questioned his words. Love. But he didn't mean *love*. Not in the Western sense, the way she knew love. He meant love as one that is familiar, important, betrothed.

After all, everyone had arranged marriages in Baraka. No one married here for love. There was a way of doing things, the bridegroom paid a *sedaq,* bride price, to the family of the bride, and the bride presented the groom a dowry, and in her case it was the ports and harbors of Melio.

"I don't know," she answered, belly tightening, nerves jumping as he continued to touch her, his hand exploring the column of her throat, the sensitive spot at the top of her spine, and now her long hair which she'd just loosened.

"You have lovely hair," he said, fingers sliding through the long strands.

"Thank you." The words stuck in her mouth.

"I'm so glad you're not a blonde. I think brunettes are much more striking," he added, holding a tendril up to the light, letting the dark brown and rich auburn highlights glimmer against his skin. He turned the long strand over. "You haven't ever wanted to be fair, have you?"

Her mouth dried. "I don't think I'd look bad as a blonde, and it's just a hair color. The face would be the same. The eyes. The nose—"

"The lips," he interrupted, covering her mouth with his in a kiss that stole her breath, turned her inside out. *This* was a kiss. This was so hot. This was so hungry and male.

Her insides felt tight. Her belly felt tense. She was achy everywhere, wanting something he was promising with his kiss but so far not delivering.

She wanted him.

All of him.

"Could you stay the night?" she whispered against his mouth, one of his hands against her breast, inflaming her nerves, her skin, her imagination.

"We were interrupted last night."

"We were," she agreed, and then remembered what had interrupted them. She felt a pang of conscience, saw Malik's expression darken. He, too, remembered. "I *am* sorry. For her, for you—"

"I appreciate your sensitivity, but in this case, you have nothing to apologize for. I've always known I could marry from within the family. The option never appealed to me." He lifted her chin, kissed her mouth, felt her lips tremble beneath his. "It will be good for her to go to America for awhile. Fatima has many family members in New York and Washington, D.C., and her immediate family knows many families. She will find the right man. I am sure of it."

Nic felt a stab of sympathy for his cousin. If Fatima truly loved Malik, she would not find him easy to forget. "I hope so," she whispered.

He circled his hands around her long hair. "We were discussing the night."

Her hands hovered at the buttons on his shirt. "Yes."

"Do I spend the night?"

"Yes." And then as she unbuttoned the first button, and the second button, she remembered one huge but crucial detail. She wasn't a natural brunette. He'd notice as soon as he saw her naked. The hair on the rest of her body was blond. *Natural* blond.

Nic's fingers were motionless now. "But if you're worried about impropriety, perhaps we just spend the night together... without making love."

"Or maybe you're worried that you can't spend a night with me without wanting to make love."

She laughed softly, embarrassed, amused. He was very funny for a sultan. Very sexy, too. "You have extraordinary confidence."

"I should. I'm very good."

This was getting quite interesting. This was the stuff she'd been dying to know. "Good, how?"

He laughed, too. "How do you think?"

"I'm supposed to be a virgin," she answered primly, ignoring the shimmering heat in her cheeks, the languid warmth throughout her body. She loved the verbal foreplay with him as much as actually touching. She loved letting the desire start with the eyes, the lips, letting words tease. She loved making love, but better than making love, was the idea that making love could be so damn fun.

"I believe Western culture has had all the virgin births it can support. You have a daughter. I'm quite sure you'll never have that virginity restored."

"So we can definitely do some things tonight, just not…everything." She'd returned to unbuttoning his shirt again. She almost had it all the way unbuttoned now, and with each button she felt her desire ratchet up another notch. "What would please you?"

His shirt fell open. He looked down at her, heat in his gaze. "You."

Nic sank down on the edge of her bed. Malik towered above her. She tried to keep from staring at the magnificent proportions of his upper body. He'd looked great in a robe last night, but in slacks and a shirt he looked…oh…unreal. "And what about me pleases you, Your Highness?"

He studied her, considered her. "Your mouth."

"My mouth."

"Your hands."

She gripped a pillow. "My hands."

"Your mind."

She wanted to throw the pillow out of the way and beg him to take her and to hell with the consequences. No one had ever liked her mind before. "You like it better than my body?" She knew she had a decent body.

"I adore your mind."

She couldn't suppress her smile. "Why?"

"It's sharp. It's smart. It's funny." His head cocked. "You're funny. I'm having a fantastic time watching you, wondering what you're going to do next. You're very daring."

What did he mean by that? What did he know? "You mean…marrying you? A stranger?"

He laughed softly, and the sound just melted Nic. She felt so hot, she pressed her knees together, pushed the pillow to her thighs.

"You'll never admit the truth, will you?"

"What truth?"

He wasn't going to answer that one. "Never mind. It's not important. I'll leave you to your sleep." Malik bent down, kissed her gently on the mouth, a long slow kiss that made Nic's head spin and tummy flip as if it'd taken flight. *"Tasbah ala khir."* Good night. Wake up happy.

"You're not going to stay?" Disappointment washed through her in waves.

"No." He sounded regretful and he kissed her again, parting her lips ever so slowly, flicking the inside of her lip with his tongue. "You wouldn't be able to keep your hands off me. And I wouldn't be able to keep my mouth off you. And I love to kiss, *laeela*. Everywhere."

Malik returned to the fire outside. Hours passed, and he couldn't make himself go to bed.

His guards wanted to stay up with him—security had been stepped up a year ago—and he knew it was for his own good, but tonight he needed space.

He reminded his guards that he was within the locked walls of the Citadel, his own fortress, a fortress that hadn't been conquered in five hundred years. "If I'm not safe here," he said to his men, "then where?"

They laughed because they were supposed to, and they retired. Finally alone, Malik's thoughts raced. He found himself thinking of not just one thing, but many, and his thoughts weren't linear.

He thought of Nicolette, his siren, and knew he'd met his match.

He thought of Fatima and her sorrow and shame, and he wished he'd known what she was expecting, wished he'd tried to find her a good match before. But she'd never wanted to marry. She'd told him many times that she'd rather stay single, than marry a stranger and leave the palace.

He thought of his younger brother, Kalen, now living in London, having studied at Oxford—just like he did—but unlike Malik, chose to sever his ties with Baraka, become a true citizen of the United Kingdom. Malik had never understood it but he'd accepted it.

But with Kalen choosing to become a U.K. citizen, he'd forfeited all rights to succession. Kalen had been second in line for the throne but now…

Malik had been furious with Kalen on moral grounds—they were Arabs, their home was North Africa—but it wasn't until the attempt on Malik's life a year ago that he understood Kalen's fears.

Kalen didn't want to get caught in politics. He wasn't a politician. He was a businessman. He thrived in the high-powered world of banking, loved the urban rush, felt like he'd found a true home in London. Malik couldn't stay angry with his brother. Every one deserved a chance to lead a happy life, a life of meaning and value. If Kalen found that meaning in London, who was he to criticize his brother?

Malik contemplated the glowing orange red fire, and knew he'd lived a good life. It'd been a very full and interesting life. He'd been blessed. And in the past several years he'd been so busy living—doing—that he'd spent very little time in contemplation.

If it weren't for the assassination attempt a year ago, he wouldn't be as contemplative as he was now.

The threat on his life last winter had forced him to become cognizant of all that he'd been given, of the blessings heaped on his head—wealth, prestige, education, power, respect. In reality, he'd been denied little. Looking back he saw that he'd lived large, loved readily and regretted nothing.

Not true, he thought, stopping himself. He did have one regret. He was sorry he'd waited so long to take a wife, start a family. He wanted a child. Needed a child. He needed an heir in case the unthinkable happened. And quite frankly, the unthinkable happened somewhere in the world every day.

A log shifted in the fire, rolling, and red-hot sparks shot up, into the still black night. Malik's eyes narrowed as he watched the sparks burn brightly then fade just as swiftly.

Life was like that, wasn't it? One was here, present, accounted for, and in those hours one had youth and life, one believed in forever.

One wanted to believe there'd be forever.

And then something happens and it changes all the naive assumptions, forces one to confront the very things human beings shy away from. Mortality.

He couldn't deny his mortality any longer. He, King Malik Roman Nuri, had a price on his head. There'd been one assassination attempt already. Malik knew there'd be another. It was simply a matter of time.

Malik crouched by the fire and stared into the shimmering red heat, letting the acrid bite of smoke waft around him, stinging his eyes, filling his nose. He could taste the smoke, feel the smoke and it reminded him of his younger days.

He'd been to battle. He'd returned from battle. He'd led his country for the past fifteen years and Baraka had benefited from his leadership, but he knew history. He'd studied history. Each man was but one part of the whole, and time was a continuum and would continue long past one man's years.

Malik knew he wasn't going to live forever, and he could accept that as long as he provided for his people. And in this case providing for them meant providing leadership. He needed a child desperately. And while the mantle of leadership would fall to his child, Malik also vowed to love his child with all his heart, and all his strength.

A rustle of fabric caught his attention and Malik turned to see Nicolette coming toward him. She was wearing one of the traditional robes, and the head covering had slipped back, exposing her chestnut hair.

"Did you ever go to bed?" she asked him, joining him at the fire.

"No," he answered, straightening.

She studied his profile for a long moment in the firelight. "Thinking of Fatima?"

He made a hoarse sound. "I'm thinking of everything."

He tipped his head back, gazed up into the sky. It was hours till dawn and the heavens were huge, endless, a dark purple punctuated by countless stars. Here in the middle of the mountains he was more nature than man. Here he was part of the wind, the sun, the sand, the air itself. He wasn't king, wasn't royal, was just a common man.

Sighing, Malik ran a hand through his hair. "I miss this life," he said at length. "I don't get away from the city often enough."

She said nothing, and he felt her watchful gaze.

"I used to spend many of my holidays here," he added, filling the silence, knowing she wanted him to speak, that she'd joined him to hear what was on his mind. "The mountains here, the red sand, it's always been special."

He turned to look at her. Her blue eyes were a clear lucid blue even now, in the middle of the night, and he thought she looked real, no longer guarded. So often she hid her emotions behind a mask, and perhaps they, royals, always did. The world was always watching so one had to be careful. But it was good to see her calm, rather contemplative, too.

"My brother and cousins also enjoyed the trips across the mountains," he added. "They liked the nights like this, when we camped out, the night spent huddled around the fire, but they've all left Baraka now. But I could never call any other place home."

"You shouldn't have to. This is your country. You were born here, raised here—"

"And you were born and raised in Melio but you're forced to leave."

Nic stood still, finding his words both painful and surprisingly honest. "I've known for awhile," she answered after a long moment. "Once we realized the situation, we all knew we'd have to leave."

"And that doesn't break your heart?"

Her eyes closed and Nic felt his deep voice seep through her, into her heart, into her veins, touching her everywhere. And that doesn't break your heart?

How could a man of his power, his position know?

How could a thirty-seven-year-old sultan understand the difficulty of the decision, of the rocky heights and depths of emotion? "One does what one must," she murmured, voice failing her and tenderness suffusing every bone and nerve.

"One could always rebel."

She shot him a swift glance. His gaze was steady, penetrating, and she felt no one had ever looked at her, or listened to her, with Malik's focus. He truly heard her. He paid attention to not just the words she said, but the meanings beneath, to all the unspoken breaths and nuances that made conversation potent. "I'm no saint. I have rebelled," she hesitated. "Many, many times."

His dark gaze traveled her face. "Yet you're here now."

Nic felt heat warm her face every place his eyes rested. He

was no ordinary man. He possessed extraordinary strength. There was nothing weak or passive about him. "I want what's best for my family."

He suddenly reached out, touched her temple with the pad of her thumb. "And not for you?"

She shivered as his thumb caressed the arch of her brow. "I need very little."

His thumb stroked along her hairline to the curve of her jaw. "You might be surprised."

Her face suddenly felt so naked, so bare—as if he'd peeled away some false self, leaving her real self exposed. She wanted him to touch her again, wanted his thumb to find her mouth, wanted his hands to frame her face, wanted him to surround her with his strength.

Bone to bone. Skin to skin.

Heart to heart.

Nic bit her lower lip, drawing the soft skin hard between her teeth.

She pulled away, turning from him. He needed a wife. He thought he'd found his queen. And yet in a matter of days she intended to leave him.

He caught her shoulders, wouldn't let her retreat. "I see the sadness in your eyes again, and last night we were interrupted, but I don't think we will be again."

"There's no sadness."

But his fingers were firm on her shoulders. "No sadness? Why, *laeela*, you have the Sahara in your eyes—endless, speechless, lonely."

"I'm not lonely." How could he read her so well? There were times it felt like he was part of her…another half of her…how could anyone—much less a man—understand her so well?

"You have been alone too long." Lowering his head, he kissed her forehead, very very gently. "I think it is the fate of being such a beautiful princess. There is no one as beautiful as you—"

"Malik."

He cupped her cheek with his hand. "Life in a high stone tower."

"No. It's not like that. I haven't lived like that. I'm not—" She broke off, swallowing hard.

"Not what?"

How to tell him that she wasn't who he believed her to be? That all his assumptions were wrong because she wasn't the good, virtuous Chantal but Nic, the one who did what she wanted to do, the one who'd taken Chantal's place to keep Malik's necessary marriage from taking place.

Everything he needed, she'd prevented.

Everything he wanted, she'd keep him from having.

This was wrong. She was wrong. Nic clasped Malik's hand, pressing his palm more tightly to her cheek. She met his gaze and in his eyes she saw kindness. Such compassion. It was almost as if he knew she harbored secrets that could hurt him, and yet he'd already forgiven her.

But it couldn't be.

He didn't know...he couldn't...*could he?*

He released her, stepped away, returning to the fire where he prodded a burning log with a stick. The log rolled over, wood popping, sparks shooting high. "So, are you going to tell me?"

There was so much to tell him. But she'd been playing the charade too long. Nic couldn't figure a way out.

"Just say it," he said coolly.

"Can we sit down?" Nic's legs had begun to shake with fear and fatigue. She knew she had to start opening up a little. She'd suffocate if she didn't.

He took a seat on the dark crimson carpet with the gold and black threads. Nic sat down near him and was relieved he didn't pull away. "I'm worried."

He waited.

Her heart pounded. She felt almost dizzy. "I'm worried about the future." The words tumbled from her lips. "I'm worried about Melio. I'm worried about my grandparents, worried about Lilly—"

"And us. You're worried about us."

"I am."

His jaw jutted. He suddenly looked very weary. "I am, too."

"You are?"

He nodded slowly. "I'm also concerned about the future."

She heard the weight of the world in his voice. Please don't

let her be the cause of his unhappiness. Please don't let her add
to his burdens. "Why?"

"I don't believe in divorce. I don't want to marry to be di-
vorced."

CHAPTER ELEVEN

HE DID doubt her, then.

"I'm not modern enough for us to marry and live apart the way some royals do," he added decisively.

Nic rubbed her fingers against the plush rug. "If we married I wouldn't want to live apart."

"*If* we married," he said, repeating her words, revealing her own noncommittal words. "You haven't made up your mind."

She wanted to protest, but her mind stayed blank and she just looked at him, wondering how on earth someone got from here to there, how chasms were crossed, oceans traveled, mountains climbed. She didn't have the strength anymore. Didn't have the courage right now, either.

The sky looked so big. The stars so high. Nic had never felt so small. Helplessly she reached for him, touching the back of his hand, her fingers sliding over his, covering them. "I want to be with you."

"Just tonight, or forever?"

If she answered honestly, and said just tonight, there'd be no tonight. If she lied and said forever, there'd be tonight but no forever.

There was no way to win this one.

He lifted his hand, pressed his fingers up against hers, and she wrapped her fingers around him. "I'm scared of marriage. It terrifies me."

"Because of Armand?"

Back to the game, the charade, the mask that Nic hated wearing. "I've just…never…wanted to be married." She couldn't be Chantal and herself any longer. She could only be herself. She could only speak for herself. "I just never fantasized about getting married, having babies. That was more Joelle and—" She broke off, swallowed and tried again. "Then I grew up, and saw that the fairy tale belongs in books. Once married, your options are limited.''

''And what are our options again?''

She marveled at his calm. ''Once you marry, you give up your freedom to choose. You don't get to be with anyone else, you have no more partners, no more different paths—''

''But how many paths do you really have, *laeela?* As a Ducasse princess, your options are limited.''

Maybe that's why she was frustrated. She didn't have the choice others had, couldn't just do what she pleased. Duty and obligation had hung over her head since birth.

''Besides,'' he continued, ''I don't feel limited. When I was younger I enjoyed being a bachelor, but I'm midway through my thirties now. I know what I want.''

''But it's not me you want. Not really.''

''But I do. Really.''

''Because of Melio, and the Mediterranean ports.''

''Initially.''

Her heart pounded, and yet she felt a disconnect from her body. ''What about me do you want?''

''Everything.''

''Because I'm a princess—''

''Because you're smart, spirited, independent, interesting.''

Nic didn't know how to reply to that. What was she supposed to think…feel? ''But you wouldn't marry me if I weren't a Ducasse.''

''And you wouldn't marry me if I weren't a Nuri.''

She was getting nowhere. ''I don't see how our marriage would work. We're both so strong and opinionated—''

''You think a marriage between a strong person and a weak person would be better? You think we're both better off with a spineless partner, one with frozen emotions?''

She searched his eyes. Did he mean it? Could he really accept her—hothead, stubborn streak, and all?

She moved to withdraw her hand and yet he wouldn't let her fingers go. ''What are you afraid of—and it's not sex. I know that much.''

Nic glanced down at their hands, fingers linked. It was good like this, comforting touching like this, but the warmth and com-

fort of joined hands could quickly become a ball and chain.
"Marriage traps a woman."

"No."

"You're a man, you don't know."

"I'm a man. And I'd never trap a woman."

Her nails dug into her palms. "It's not even a choice men
make. It just happens. Marriage…motherhood…children. It
changes a woman. Your priorities change…they must change."

The heat in his eyes burned her. He stared at her so intensely
it made her almost dizzy. "Is that such a bad thing?"

"It is if you value your freedom."

"And your freedom is so valuable?"

Nic was finding it harder and harder to breathe. The air felt
heavy, close, pressing in on them. He didn't understand, he
hadn't seen what she'd seen—her mother's career ended, her
incredible voice and talent hidden from the world, her energy
devoted to supporting her father's efforts, and then Chantal,
locked away in a chateau in La Croix, trapped. Ignored. Lied
to. "It is to me."

She looked away, remembering the delicate gold birdcage
she'd seen earlier in the day with the pretty orange and yellow
birds inside. Her heart had gone out to the tiny songbirds. It'd
kill her to become what Chantal had become. She'd rather die
than be trampled by a person she'd trusted…

"You'd clip my wings," she whispered, feeling tears start to
thicken her throat. "I'd hate it." She swallowed the threat of
tears. "And I'd hate you for it."

He brought her hand to his mouth, kissed her curled fingers.
"Hate is such a strong word."

She looked at him, her chest tightened, heart knotted. "Hate
is such a strong feeling."

He released her hand and leaned back, letting the fire warm
him. "You know hate, then?"

Her nerves were frayed. She'd said things she'd never intended to say. "I did love someone once," she said after a long
moment's silence. "And it couldn't work. Denying the love was
so hard. It did something to me. Broke something in me."

"Your heart," he supplied softly.

Nic shrugged uneasily. She didn't believe much in romance
and Valentines, and no one had ever said life would be simple,

but she'd never expected it to get so challenging so quickly, either. "Getting over Daniel took me years. Forgetting a love doesn't happen all at once. I had to work at it, over and over. There were days I didn't think I'd make it without picking up the phone and calling him."

"Did you pick up the phone?"

"No. But I wanted to." She closed her eyes. *Badly.*

"What happened?"

"By the second year I'd learned to ride the pain out. And date like mad. I must have been out every night of the week." She had to make him understand, had to get him to see. "I'm not innocent anymore. I've lived enough to know the way the world works, how relationships evolve. Sooner or later you'd want me to be something, someone, other than I am."

"Maybe you did have a bad first marriage, but your parents—they were happy. Everyone knows they were extremely close."

Nic flexed her fingers. "Mom shouldn't have given up her career. It shouldn't have happened."

"It would have been difficult for her to tour, be with your father, and have a family."

"*Exactly.*" She shook her head. "And you might not think it now, or know it now, but eventually I wouldn't be what you wanted. I wouldn't be what you needed. You'd try to change me. It happens all the time. People fall in love with one thing, but eventually its not enough—" She broke off.

Malik studied her for a long moment before getting to his feet, and tugged her up, too. "We need a change of scenery. Come."

The Citadel's Moorish doorways were horseshoe shaped, dramatic arches carved of wood and stone, ornate lattice work and elegant filigree. Each of the arches in the fortress was unique and when Malik led her through a doorway into a bedroom, Nicolette froze.

Candles flickered on the low round table by the bed, in the sconces on the wall, in the niches tucked around the opulent bedroom.

"Where are we?" she asked, watching Malik deliberately close the thick dark wood doors, locking the latch.

"My bedroom."

He pressed her against the wall, his hands framing her face

then sliding through her hair, his fingers threading between the long silky strands. "I want you." His voice sounded rough with desire. "And you can trust me, *laeela*. I won't let you down."

Nic swallowed, holding the tears back. He was talking about Armand. He was referring to the horrible life Chantal had led in La Croix but he didn't understand that she wasn't that woman. Compared to Chantal, Nic had had it easy. Her life was uncomplicated.

But she couldn't hold back the rush of emotion. She loved the feel of his chest against hers, loved the strength of his ribs and hips. He was hard—nearly as hard as the wall—and she loved being caught like this, loved being covered like this, her body hidden from all, reserved for just him.

She lifted her lips, wanting to feel him take her mouth.

Wanting to feel him take her—finally.

She was such a strong person, so determined, and yet despite all her strength and drive, she yearned to feel a connection with another. And she felt that bond with him.

He kissed her, covering her mouth with his, and with his hands braced on either side of her head she felt his body brush hers, a slow, lazy contact that left her craving more. She pressed up against his long torso, bringing her hips to meet his, sighing with pleasure when she felt the hard ridge in his trousers.

Malik lifted his head, lips curving wryly. "Do all men feel this way about you?" he asked, even as his hand trailed down one loose tendril of hair, across her shoulder, over her collarbone, to the peak of her breast.

"Like how?"

"Like they can't live without you." His palm covered her right breast, her sensitive nipple hidden in the palm of his hand. "As if life wouldn't be worth anything if you weren't there."

Nic swallowed, trying to think when her body was melting, sending conflicting signals to her brain. Desire, hunger…so hard to stay focused on the practical and the plan. "I don't think that's the common response men have to me, no."

"What about the one you loved all those years ago? What was his name?"

He was kneading her breast, fingers playing the soft tissue. She forced her fuzzy brain to clear. "Daniel?"

"Yes."

She tried not to gasp as he leaned into her, his knee parting her thighs and she felt his hard thigh press against the apex of her legs, heightening sensation not just there, but everywhere.

She might as well have been naked. His skin was so warm against hers, she felt her temperature rise, hotter and hotter and as his hand caressed the length of her, shaping from her breast to her waist, hip, and back again she thought she'd go up in flames any moment.

Nic shivered as his hand returned to her breast, his fingers burning through her thin *jellaba*, her breast aching in his hand, the nipple hard and sensitive. Pressed as she was to the wall, his hips held her still so each caress of his fingers made her dance against him, shuddering with pleasure.

She could feel his heat and strength throughout her body. She'd become a dancing girl, trembling against him, arching helplessly, needing more than just his hands on her breasts, wanting his hands on naked skin—her belly, her hips, between her legs. She wrapped her arms around his shoulders, drew him closer. "Blow out the candles," she begged in his ear. "Blow out the candles and let's just be together."

He stripped her in the dark, leisurely removing each item, not that they were difficult to take off. She was wearing only her thin cotton nightgown covered by the modest *jellaba*. But in the dark, with Malik's hands slowly wandering over her, Nic felt as if she wore gold and silk threads, gossamer fabrics of great beauty.

She didn't speak. He didn't speak, and his touch was that of a man who had infinite time. His whole pleasure seemed centered on exploring her, hands lightly caressing the curves of her body. His lips followed his hands, his mouth brushing across her heated skin savoring her softness, her warmth, her texture.

When he knelt at her feet, she took a step backwards. "Not that," she protested. "Not yet."

He kissed the inside of her thigh. "I'm not doing that. Not yet."

She felt his smile against her thigh and it made her smile. She knew him so well already, could picture his silent amusement, the tolerant gleam in his eye. His confidence knew no end.

With him kneeling at her feet, his hands traced the line of her leg, from the curve of her buttock, to the indentation where cheek met thigh, and down the back of her thighs to her knees. His fingertips drew invisible patterns at the back of her knees and then inside her kneecaps, light deft strokes that made her feel so hollow on the inside, and then his hands were teasing down her shins, circling her ankles, finding her sensitive insteps and between her toes.

By the time he'd reached her toes she felt as if she were humming with energy. She felt deliciously awake, her senses alert. Eager.

Standing, Malik stripped off his clothes and reaching for Nicolette, pulled her into his arms, letting their warm naked bodies just touch, and Nic drew a small breath, responding to the brush of his body against hers, aware of things she might not have felt if the lights had been on. She felt the smooth hard plane of his chest, the way his hip bone pressed against her skin, the silky hair at the juncture of his legs. He was so firm, and strong, and she loved the way she fit against him, loved how his arms wrapped around her.

When he lifted her into his arms and headed for the bed, Nic pressed her face to his neck and inhaled the spicy scent of the fragrance sill lingering on his warm skin. His biceps pressed against her soft breast, his hand clasped her naked bottom, and desire shot through her, sharp, intense, demanding.

He placed her in the middle of his enormous bed, but Nic didn't lie passively beneath him. She encircled his shoulders, drew him down to her, felt the rigid length of him nudge her thighs even as she offered him her mouth. His jaw scraped across her skin, the new growth of his beard making her own skin feel raw, and with the cool silk coverlet beneath her heated skin, she felt incredibly wanton.

In the dark, with her sight denied, all the other senses became highly tuned. She could smell the smoke of the fire in his hair, taste the mint of tea on his breath, feel the firm satin texture of his skin, and the dense, thick muscle.

He didn't even need to ask her to do anything. As his hard body touched hers, she opened her legs for him, wanting to be with him, thinking nothing had ever been more natural in her life.

He filled her slowly, entering her with remarkable control, ensuring she had plenty of time to adjust to his size. Nic hadn't realized he was so well endowed until the sense of fullness was almost overwhelming.

Her breath caught in her throat, and she wrapped her fingers around his upper arms trying to make this easier. Malik kissed her slowly. His tongued traced her lips, teasing the swollen lower lip, and as her body relaxed, he clasped her bottom, lifting her hips, allowing her to better accommodate him.

He moved slowly, his muscles sleek beneath her hands. He sank into her, deep, steady strokes, each thrust of his narrow hips powerful yet controlled. She loved the feel of him, relished his languid grace, the warmth of his skin, the satiny texture of his lower back and buttocks.

He already seemed to understand her body intimately, touching her with deft skill, taking his time in building the tension. She was grateful he didn't race to a conclusion, grateful that he, too, seemed to find their joining ultimately satisfying, and yet the friction of their bodies settled into a rhythm satisfying and yet not, because the pleasure demanded more. Each thrust into her made her need another. She met his driving hips, lifting up to meet him, push against him and the tension built.

"Slow," she whispered, fingers kneading his shoulders. "Slow. I don't want this to—"

She broke off, closed her eyes, trying to stop the first tremor, not wanting to reach orgasm yet, not wanting anything about this amazing night to end, but her muscles were wound too tight, the nerves stretched, and his deep thrusting pushed her ever closer to the brink of no return.

Nic kissed Malik with near desperation. She wished she could tell him how right this felt, how as crazy as it sounded, everything about them made sense to her. She'd never felt so right with anyone before. But it was impossible to speak. Words were impossible. He was claiming her, his body demanding her. He buried himself in her, harder, faster, a silent possession which sent Nicolette over the edge, shattering, one intense contraction after another.

Malik came even as she did, and she felt his hard body surge and shudder in her arms, his jaw clenched as he struggled to contain his passion. Tears came to her eyes as she held him tightly, wrapping her arms more closely around his shoulders, listening to the fierce pounding of his heart beneath her ear. His body still throbbed inside hers, making her own body pulse in small aftershocks of pleasure. It was such simple lovemaking, she thought, kissing his chest, right above his heart, and yet it was the most satisfying experience she'd ever known.

Malik shifted, turning them both so she lay cradled against his chest. They lay like that for long minutes, utterly quiet.

Malik's royal bedchamber was dark and yet in the dark Nicolette saw colors she'd never seen before. Making love with him had been everything she'd ever wanted, and more. She'd never felt this close to anyone, nor so loved. When he was in her, part of her, she truly felt as if they were one.

With her cheek resting on his chest, she let the steady beat of his heart sink into every bone and muscle, and the peace stayed with her. The minutes stretched. She exhaled slowly, inhaled, exhaled again, and she thought just maybe everything was going to work out.

Nic felt like talking, really talking. Usually after sex she just wanted to get up, shower and put her clothes on. It wasn't that sex had ever been bad, but afterward, she hadn't felt comfortable with the intimacy part. But that was different now. She wanted to know everything he thought. Wanted to feel what he felt.

"Was that okay?" she whispered tentatively.

She felt a rumble in his chest. "Yes," he answered. "Was it okay for you?"

She sighed and smiled in the dark. "I thought it was amazing. I've never felt anything like that before."

"I'm glad it gave you pleasure." He stretched a little. Their bodies were still damp and her long hair fell in a tangled heap across his chest.

Nic pushed up on one elbow, looked down at Malik and even though it was dark she wanted to face him, feel his breath, be close to him. "It wasn't just pleasure, it was...more. You gave me..." She didn't even know how to explain it, but what they did, what they were together was perfect. Nothing had ever felt more right in her life.

"Yes?"

But she couldn't find the words. Instead she bent her head, found his mouth, kissed him tenderly, and as her lips teased his, she touched his cheek, feeling the sharp bristles of his beard along his jawbone.

"You're beautiful," she whispered wonderingly, letting her hand slide down his jaw, to his chest, her nails dragging lightly across his nipple and the unyielding muscle.

"I'm not."

"You are."

"My nose is too big," he complained, palming the fullness of her breasts, playing her nipples until they pebbled in his hands.

She felt her womb clench, flooding her body with warmth. "It's not," she whispered, trying to ignore the electric current running through her, the dampness between her legs, the fierce desire building all over again.

"My mouth's too wide," he added, cupping her bottom in his hands and pulling her back on top of him.

She shuddered at the rigid feel of him. He'd recovered already and his erection pressed between her thighs, the thick tip already sliding against her warm slick flesh. "The best lips I've ever kissed," she murmured hoarsely.

"And the last lips you'll kiss," he answered, wrapping his hands around her thighs, and parting her wide.

Even in the dark Nic gasped. Gripping his shoulders, her thighs spread wide in his hands, she could do nothing to stop him from enjoying her his way.

He was so naturally sensual, so comfortable with bodies and the physical, that as he rubbed her naked, sensitized flesh against his rigid shaft she felt as if there was a whole world of lovemaking she knew nothing about. His touch demanded trust. His skill was far beyond anything she'd ever known before.

Again he let his erection slide across her wetness, and she closed her eyes, seeing bright sparks, the pleasure and sensation so intense. She could feel the straining tip, the warm silken head running along her cleft, and she squirmed, trying to take him, wanting to take him. Once, twice, his swollen shaft slid across her opening, teasing her where she was so moist and pliant.

But he wouldn't enter her. His lips brushed her bare shoulder. His fingers kneaded her thighs, parting her wider and wider until she thought she'd break.

"What are you doing to me?" she demanded, panting.

"I was just remembering a conversation," he said, one hand leaving her thigh to reach between their bodies. He found the damp heat of her. Slowly he slid one finger into her core, which felt as if it had come alive, pulsing around his finger. Yet the slow thrust of his finger gave no relief. The slow, tantalizing touch only crazed her senses.

"Do you remember our conversation about men, women and sex?" he continued, turning his finger slightly, stirring every possible nerve ending.

Nic bucked against his hand. She needed more. God, she needed more. "No."

"You were saying that in your experience—"

"I can't talk," she interrupted hoarsely, as he slid his finger out of her warm body, and she felt utterly lost, completely bereft. "I can't even think."

He lifted her up by the rib cage, holding her torso above him, and his lips found her navel, and he licked his way from her belly button to her sternum, completely avoiding her breasts. "I'll help you then. You were telling me, I believe," he said, letting the air cool her damp hot skin, "that most men have no idea how to touch a woman."

Nic squeezed her eyes shut. Oh dear God, not this, not now. Not that conversation.

He arched her backward, bending her back at the waist and as he did so, his hard shaft thrust against her exposed flesh, the delicate bud so ripe it hurt.

"You were saying men had no idea what women wanted—"

"Malik!"

He stroked the rigid length of him against her tender flesh over and over. "Now help me, Princess," he said stunningly conversational. "Just where is this clitoris?"

My God. He was going to melt her brain. She was losing it. She burned and throbbed everywhere. Her skin felt hot and she felt desperate. "I eat my words," she choked. *"Please."*

And then the tip of his finger found her, right at the sweet spot between her legs. "Am I getting close?"

"Stop talking," she gasped, breathing shallowly in great gulps of air. His touch was exquisite. That delicious play of his finger.

He stopped touching her. "I'm afraid I don't know what to do—"

She leaned over him, covered his mouth in a desperate kiss.

"You do know, you're doing it, please Malik, please, you're making me mad."

He kissed her back, drawing the tip of her tongue into his mouth, and sucking on the tip, tight hard rhythmic sucks that had her swinging her hips.

And then catching her hips, he plunged into her, hard, deep, burying himself in her tight sheath and she cried out, and he pulled her against him, so that her nipples rubbed against the crisp hair of his chest and his hard abdomen pressed to her naked belly and the heat was intense, the heat inside her an inferno. She was so hot, so wet she was melting inside. She gave up, gave her body to him, gave the rest of her resistance, too.

He'd captured her whole—heart, mind, body and soul—and the orgasm was spectacular, but nothing like the release of control.

She'd found love. She'd found the other half of her soul.

Nic didn't remember falling asleep after they'd made love the second time. She didn't remember anything but the joy and comfort of being in Malik's arms. But when she woke, dawn was breaking, a pale blue skin beyond the shuttered window.

She stirred sleepily and Malik kissed the top of her head.

"You're mine now," he said, his deep voice gruff. "You're only mine."

"Mmmm," she agreed, snuggling closer. "I know."

He stroked her hip beneath the light silk coverlet. "No more maybe about the wedding."

"No." And then it was like a massive stone fortress breaking. Nic saw light, way down at the end of the tunnel. There was no reason not to marry Malik. She should just do it. It was the right thing for everyone—Melio, the country's economy, her family. "I'm glad we're getting married in six days." She curled against him, "It's just six days, isn't it?"

"Five now."

"Sounds good." She lifted her face, brushed her mouth across his chin and sighed when he found her lips, kissed her deeply. "It'll be nice to get it over with."

"You're sure?"

"Yes." And wrapped in his arms, Nic pictured the ceremony they'd have in Atiq. She'd wear one of the new gowns made for her, and Malik would look gorgeous no matter what he wore and the whole picture felt right.

Except for one little but crucial detail. Lilly.

"I want Lilly here," Nic said, clasping Malik's arm, needing to feel his strength. "She has to be here."

"She will be."

"Her grandparents, the Thibaudets, might not let her—"

"They will." He kissed the top of her head. "Don't worry, *laeela.* I'll take care of everything."

CHAPTER TWELVE

NIC stretched, rolling onto her side with a deeply contented sigh of pleasure. Now that was brilliant sex. Just one night and Malik had spoiled her forever.

Opening her eyes she discovered Malik standing, arms crossed, watching her from the front of the bed.

She sat up, combed her long hair back, the covers at her waist. "You're dressed."

"I've been in my office working the past couple hours but I returned to have breakfast in bed."

His expression made her breath catch in her throat. "Are we talking orange juice and scrambled eggs?" But her body was already responding, her bare breasts tingling, the nipples peaking.

His gaze rested on her full breasts. "Sure."

She felt heat rise through her, a blush that pinked her skin from head to toe. "I mean, on a *plate*."

His deep laugh echoed, the sexy husky sound coiling in her tummy, making her feel hotter, emptier. She could almost feel his hands on her, his hard body slowly filling her, all silky heat and strength until she was dissolving around him. Pleasure. Endless pleasure, endless sensation.

"If you insist," he mocked, moving to ring for the breakfast tray. It arrived minutes later and Malik took the tray from the male steward, carrying the tray to the bed where Nic waited.

Malik lounged on the bed next to her, his powerful body at ease and cradling her coffee, Nic felt as if the night had been one long, sexual dream. The lovemaking had reached a level of eroticism Nic had never experienced before, and yet it had felt completely natural, too.

"How do you feel?" he asked, popping a miniature almond and apricot pastry into his mouth.

The muscles deep inside her clenched. He was more man than

149

ten men together. Again heat swept through her, burning her. "Fine. Thank you."

He lay on his side, his elbow propping his weight. "Have you changed your mind about the wedding?"

"No. Have you?"

He laughed once. "I knew I shouldn't have gotten intimate with you. Now you'll have forever confused love and sex."

Nic nearly rolled her eyes. "I've never confused love and sex before."

"Yes, but was the sex that good before?"

Blushing all over again, Nic gave him a reproving look. "No one's ever made me beg before."

"I withheld nothing."

Her blush deepened. No, he had not. He gave her every-thing—and more.

"I want you." His voice suddenly dropped, throbbing with raw naked need. "I want you like you won't believe. What I feel for you—what I want to do with you—" He shook his head, warningly. "This is dangerous, *laeela*."

She couldn't breathe. She wanted him in her, now, filling her. She felt fierce, demanding, her body all melting need, a need that could only be answered by him. "You might be right about that."

His hungry gaze held hers. "I had an idea."

"Yes?"

"I think we should get married in Melio."

It was the last thing she'd expected him to say. "Marry...in Melio?"

"You could have your family with you—"

"I thought we were going to have just a traditional wedding here. You know, televise the ceremony, big national holiday."

"We'll just broadcast the ceremony from there."

Panic raced through her. "It'd be too much of a strain on my family. My grandparents aren't well—"

"Which is why we'd go there. There'd be no traveling for your family. The cathedral is just down the street from the pal-ace."

She leaned forward, planted a desperate kiss on his lips, trying to distract him. "We can see them later...after our honeymoon.

Really, Malik, let's not complicate things. It'd be too much fuss. Royal weddings are such big deals in Europe.''

He wasn't to be distracted. ''Perhaps we ought to think about your grandparents' needs. I know how it feels to worry about one's family. I know what a comfort it is when you know that your family is looked after, and I know it'd greatly reassure your grandfather to know that while ours is an arranged marriage, it isn't cold, or unbearable.''

Did he even know what he was doing? ''There would be so many preparations.''

''Taken care of.''

Her mouth dry, she reached for her juice glass off the tray and sipped slowly, trying to give her mind a chance to clear. ''What do you mean…taken care of?''

''As I said to your grandfather earlier—''

''What?''

He wrapped his hand around hers, securing the glass in her fingers. ''You better drink. You look pale.''

But she couldn't drink. She couldn't think.

He urged the glass to her lips, tilted it against her mouth. ''You need some sugar. Drink up. I don't want you fainting on me now, not when we've so much to do before we fly out.''

Nic nearly bit through the glass. She forced herself to swallow one mouthful before she pushed the glass away. ''I don't understand any of this.''

''You're a widow, not a divorcee. You're entitled to a lavish second wedding, and so this morning, after waking I've been on the phone. I called your grandfather first, and then had my office staff begin shifting all wedding arrangements from Atiq to Porto Terza.''

He'd called Grandfather…

Nic blinked. ''What did you say to him?''

''That you were here, and you'd agreed to marry me—''

''Who did you tell him I was?''

Malik looked at her as if she'd lost her mind. ''Who do you think?''

She reached for her juice, slurped it down, and wiping off her mouth she looked up at him. ''You told him I was Chantal.''

''Yes.''

''And Grandpapa said…?''

"That no, you couldn't be Chantal because Chantal was in La Croix. He'd just spoken to her a few minutes earlier."

Nic's eyes searched his. "Malik?"

"Yes, *laeela?*"

"What are you thinking right now?"

"That I have an imposter princess."

Pretty accurate description. She set her glass down very carefully. Thank goodness he wasn't getting angry. She didn't think she could have handled that on top of all this. "I am a Ducasse princess."

"But not Chantal."

"No." He smiled at her, rather pleasantly actually, considering the circumstances.

Her stomach felt funny. She'd drunk the juice too fast, maybe. "I'm…"

"Nicolette."

She nodded awkwardly. "How'd you guess?"

His black eyebrows lifted. "Are you serious?"

"I just thought…"

"We've spent the night together. It's been pretty intimate, but that's not how I knew." He hesitated and her heart lurched sickeningly. "I've always known," he admitted. "From the moment you arrived."

"What?"

"I've spoken with the real Chantal on the phone before. You're smart, Nic, and you're beautiful, but you're nothing like your older sister."

She lay back on the bed, dragged the covers to her shoulders, and stared at the ceiling. "That's why you called grandfather."

"He knew you were here all along."

"Just like you did." She squeezed her eyes shut. This was just getting worse and worse. "Why didn't you confront me? Why didn't you make me confess the truth?"

His laughter drifted over. "I was…amused. I found your charade entertaining."

He didn't just say that. He couldn't have just meant that. She'd been in emotional turmoil and he'd been having fun? "So what happens now?"

"We go to Melio and get married."

"You still want to get married?"

He made a rough sound, impatient, disbelieving. *"Yes."*

"What else did he say, my grandfather?"

"That you had it coming." Malik's laughter was soft, goading. "He said to remind you that he'd once said—"

"I'd meet my match." She opened her eyes again, feeling as if she were riding a roller coaster. What was happening? How had everything turned so fast? Her head was spinning. "Maybe we could just stay here and skip the big wedding."

"Skip the wedding?"

"I'll be your mistress."

The covers came flying off her and Malik loomed over her, his expression incredulous. Malik, for all his sensuality, was quite old-fashioned. "You didn't just say that."

She felt a quiver shoot through her. "Our children could still be your heirs."

"Make a princess a mistress?" he drawled derisively. "I don't think so."

She'd always been such a truthful person. All her life she'd pushed at the limits, refused to accept the boundaries, but at least she'd always been honest. "You wanted Chantal."

"But I've made love to Nic."

She shook on the inside, and she realized she hadn't just been lying to him. She'd been lying to herself. She loved him. She'd fallen in love with him.

"Malik." She hadn't realized she'd even spoken his name aloud until he reached for her, lowering the weight of his body, his hips and chest covering the naked length of her. She shuddered at the pleasure of his body on hers and closed her eyes, overwhelmed by everything. She'd fallen for him. So hard.

But how?

Opening her eyes she looked into his silver gaze, the cool depth lit by a small silent smile, she knew how.

He was amazing. Gorgeous and physical, sexual and sensual, he was smart. And patient. Tolerant.

"You don't have to marry me just because we made love," she said, her voice hoarse.

He kissed the side of her neck. "You're still running away."

"No."

"You can't run."

"I can." But her voice wobbled.

Looking down at her, his eyes warmed to hot liquid silver. "You can't," he chided gently. "I won't let you go."

But she knew those were just words. He was teasing her, playing with her. Enjoying her.

And God, he did enjoy her, didn't he? She felt it in every nerve and fiber of her body. She felt his humor and pleasure, felt his interest, felt his concern. He would always do what was best for her. He might say he'd never let her go, but if she wanted out, wanted to leave, he'd never keep her with him against her will.

"I never planned on getting married." It felt as if the words were wrung from her. "I never planned on staying in Baraka."

His smile faded and he shifted his weight, moving off of her. "I know."

They spent the rest of the day apart, even had their meals alone, but late that evening Malik came to her bed and his kiss was hard, possessive, territorial. Malik stretched her out beneath him and she felt the volatility of their emotions in the intensity of their lovemaking. He wanted her, and he wanted her to know that there was no way in hell he was letting her go.

Two days later they returned to Atiq, but they weren't staying for more than a few hours. Malik was giving her time to pack and then they'd be off, heading to Melio where her family was waiting.

In her room, Nic asked Alea for help. "I need a really good hair stylist," Nic said, telling Alea exactly what she intended to do. Alea looked horrified but Nic felt calm. Malik knew who she was. It was time to become a blonde again. Nic was more than ready to rinse all signs of Chantal away.

Nic wore a robe and head covering on the way to the airport. She wasn't ready to shock all of Malik's household staff. Let Alea pass the word while Nic was in Melio.

They boarded on schedule, and Malik's royal jet took off from Atiq's airport at two in the afternoon. The flight from Atiq to Porto Terza in Melio would take about three and a half hours but three and a half hours sounded like forever to Nic right now.

They'd only been in the air a few minutes when Malik leaned

forward and tugged the head covering off. "Can I see what my fiancée looks like?"

She silently endured Malik's inspection. His intense examination reminded her of her first day in Baraka, when he'd circled her twice, studying her from head to toe. "Do I pass?"

"Is that your natural color?"

"You don't like it."

"You're very blond."

She turned her head, stared out the window biting her lip. But she couldn't keep her temper in check. "You don't have to marry me."

"You could already be pregnant."

What kind of answer was that? "Well, don't do me any favors!"

He surprised her by laughing. "I won't." His laughter faded and still studying her, he asked, "Does Daniel still work in the palace garage?"

"Yes, why?" Nic blinked in surprise. "And how did you remember his name?"

"I'm very good with names." He gave her a long, level look. "Do you still love him?" Malik's silver gaze was no longer cool. He seethed with emotion.

"No. I don't love him. I'm marrying you."

"Do you love me?"

She pointedly held his burning gaze. "Do you love me?"

He said nothing. He just looked at her as if he knew her, and understood her. He looked so kindly and intently that she felt hot sparks shoot through her belly, into her veins.

He wanted her. He loved her. Maybe he hadn't said *I, Malik Roman Nuri, love you,* but the words, it was there in his body, in his eyes, in his heart.

He might not even use the word love in the Western sense, but the emotion she saw in his eyes was the emotion she wanted to feel when the man she loved looked at her.

She felt a surge of raw emotion so strong it hurt.

Malik unbuckled his seat belt. "Let's get something to drink from the bar. I think we both need to relax."

Three hours later the jet circled once over Porto Terza before making its final descent.

Safely buckled back in her seat, Nic's breath caught in her

throat as she gazed at Porto Terza from the air. In the late afternoon sunlight, the ocean gleamed purple and turquoise, the surface of the water sparkling in sheets of silver white, and Porto Terza's historic buildings shone a rich creamy beige against cliffs of dark green. *Melio*.

Nic suddenly reached for Malik's hand. "I'm nervous."

He grimaced. "You're not alone, princess. I am, too."

The plane's wheels touched the tarmac and settled into a smooth taxi down the length of the private runway. They'd arrived at the Ducasse family's airport, a small terminal reserved for the royal family and visiting dignitaries, and Nic's insides were turning over again. She couldn't pretend it was excitement or happiness. It was dread. And fear. She'd come home to Melio to marry—a sultan, no less.

A chauffeured Mercedes sedan waited at the airport for them. Within minutes they were entering the palace gates and sweeping up the grand driveway, shaded by palm trees planted over a hundred years ago.

The palace was a graceful stone building with a Palladian entrance, a domed center court, and elegant wings flanking either side. Massive marble lions guarded the front door and Nic shot Malik a nervous smile as they climbed the front steps. "This is home," she said, nodding at the navy uniformed staff members who'd quickly assembled in the hall to greet them.

Malik took a moment to gaze around the grand entrance. The Porto Terza palace was smaller than many European palaces, and yet the charm lay in its style and scale. Although the central staircase was quite grand, and all the floors and columns were two shades of marble—pink and gold—the palace interior was sunny and warm like the late afternoon sunshine outside.

Footsteps sounded above, and Joelle appeared at the top of the stairs. "Nicolette!" She dashed down the stairs and threw her arms around her sister, whispering in her ear. "You've got everybody in an uproar. What have you done?"

"I don't know," Nic answered weakly.

Joelle drew back, studied Nic's face. "You're really getting married?"

Nic didn't know whether to laugh or cry. She turned, gestured to Malik. "Joelle, the groom's right here."

There were endless introductions for the rest of the evening.

A private predinner reception with Nic's grandparents, King Remi and Queen Astrid, and then a massive sit down dinner with nearly all of the King's advisors. Nic had no chance to be alone with Malik. Her grandfather kept Malik firmly at his side.

Nic went to sit with Queen Astrid once dishes were cleared and everyone was free to informally socialize. "Are you angry with me, Grandmama?" she asked nervously.

Her grandmother's stroke last year had made it difficult for her to speak, but she managed a small smile. "No," Queen Astrid mouthed. "Grandpapa and I know you."

The next morning Nic woke and her first thought was that there'd been no word from Chantal. The wedding was in two days.

Where was she? Why weren't she and Lilly here? They were supposed to be here. Her grandfather said Chantal had planned on leaving with Lilly yesterday to help Nic with last minute wedding details. But Chantal hadn't arrived and Nic went in search of answers.

Grandfather was worse than no help. He was the bearer of bad news. "They're not going to make it," he said, motioning for Nic to move from the doorway and sit in his private office. "I didn't want to upset you yesterday, not when it was King Nuri's first day here, but apparently the Thibaudets don't think it's wise for Lilly to travel so far for such a short period of time."

Nic felt the old anger return. It was all she could do to keep her voice quiet. "Then let her come for a couple of weeks! Lilly hasn't been home to Porto Terza in nearly two years. It was all she could do to keep her voice quiet. *Two* years, Grandpapa. Don't you want to see her?"

"Of course I do."

"Then call King Phillipe, tell him you and Grandmama insist that Lilly come—"

"The child's not well, Nicolette."

Tears started to form in Nic's eyes. "If she's not well it's because La Croix is bad for her! All I ever hear is how fragile Lilly is, how small and delicate for her age. Maybe she needs someone to get her out of there."

"You're being overly dramatic."

Nic stared at him, not understanding how he could ignore the facts. He hadn't seen his granddaughter in fourteen months. He and Grandmama had gone to La Croix to visit Chantal and Lilly a couple months before Lilly's third birthday. Well Lilly was four now. And her grandparents who were just an hour and a half away by plane had had no visit since then.

Was he afraid of the truth? Did it make him feel helpless, powerless, or was he just too tired to face the reality anymore? "The Thibaudets have taken over her life. Chantal has little say in Lilly's upbringing. They've pushed Chantal out—"

"This isn't right. I don't like this." He stood up, leaned on a corner of his desk. "You mustn't speak of Phillipe and Catherine this way. I've known the Thibaudets my whole life. Queen Catherine and your grandmother were close, childhood friends."

Nic swallowed the lump lodged in her throat. "That doesn't mean—" She broke off as her grandfather headed to the window, walking slowly, virtually turning his back on her. He'd aged a decade in the past year. She couldn't stand it.

"I'm going to bring her home, Grandpapa. You don't have to like it. You don't have to agree. You just can't stop me."

CHAPTER THIRTEEN

NIC found Malik in a palace salon with a large group of security experts—Porto Terza's chief of police, the captain from the palace guard, plain-clothes detectives, secret service agents from a half dozen foreign countries.

Apparently all of Europe was showing up. Kings, queens, prince, princesses, duke and duchesses. There were political leaders from every superpower, industry leaders from the business sector, fashion scions, celebrities with connections, even the American president's wife had just flown in and was staying at the Porto Palace Hotel, Melio's revered five star hotel property.

Joelle had said that with the ceremony taking place at the palace, and the reception in the Porto Palace Hotel's grand ballroom, the sultan was taking no chance with security and she'd been right. Malik was taking no chances.

She listened as Malik conversed with the blond American secret service agent, the American's strong Texas twang giving away his place of birth. It boggled Nic's mind—a Cathedral wedding with Cardinal Juneau presiding followed by a reception for five hundred at the Palace Hotel...

It was enough to make her want to grab her *jellaba* and run for the desert. Instead Nic stepped from the shadows, caught Malik's eye and indicated she needed to speak with him.

He joined her in the hall a few minutes later. "What's happened?" he asked, immediately seeing the stress in her face.

Nic explained quickly. She left nothing out. Due to some archaic La Croix law, Chantal couldn't take Princess Lilly, heir to the throne, out of the country without the King and Queen's permission, and The Thibaudets weren't going to let Lilly come.

She also explained her grandfather's position on it, and how he—who had the power to challenge the Thibaudets—refused to do so. After she'd told him everything she felt the weight return, the heaviness of her heart that had been there for so long now.

She didn't want to hurt or humiliate Malik, but she also knew herself. She couldn't forget what had taken her to Baraka in the first place.

"I went to Baraka to free Lilly." Her heart felt so bruised she could barely look at him. "The only reason I pretended to be Chantal was to find a way to get Lilly out of La Croix. I can't marry you if she isn't here. I made her a *promise*."

He said nothing, his expression calm, unruffled as always.

"I'm asking you to help bring her home for the wedding." Her eyes were gritty and her throat felt raw. "I don't want to say I won't marry you. I don't want to humiliate you. But she has to be here. That was my goal, Malik, that was my objective all along."

"And I assured you that she would be."

"But that was before—"

"Nothing's changed. I gave you my word."

But the morning of the wedding arrived and Nic woke, heart sick. Chantal wasn't here. Lilly wasn't here. Malik was completely uncommunicative. Whenever she asked about Chantal and Lilly, he simply said, "I'm doing everything I can possibly do."

But what exactly did that entail? What had he done? What hadn't he done? And if he was working so hard on getting them here, why weren't they?

It made Nic crazy. She wanted to jump on a plane with the palace guard, fly into La Croix and scoop up Lilly and Chantal and bring them home.

A knock sounded on Nic's bedroom door and Joelle's dark head appeared around the corner. "I've got coffee."

"Then you can come in."

Joelle carried two cups of steaming café au lait to the bed. "You're not up yet?"

"Don't start," Nic groaned, pushing herself into a sitting position. "You sound just like Alea."

Joelle grinned. "I know." She handed Nic her coffee before taking a seat on the foot of the bed. "You've told me all about her. She sounds great."

Nic was going to say something sarcastic but inexplicably her eyes filled with tears.

Joelle's smile disappeared. "Chantal would be here if she could," she said softly, knowing exactly what Nic was thinking. "But you can't let Chantal's absence ruin your day. This is your wedding day—"

"No. It's not." Nic set her coffee down on the night stand. "I'm not getting married."

"*Nic.*"

"I can't."

"Nic, he's great. It may have been an arranged marriage, but he's…gorgeous, and sexy and—" her hand gestured as she struggled for words "*—perfect* for you."

"It doesn't matter." She slid from the bed, reached for her old white woven robe. It was a super soft cotton robe she'd had forever and simply loved. "And don't look at me like that. Malik knows."

"Does he?"

Nic nodded and swallowed, but on the inside, she wasn't so sure. Malik had to know she was serious. She wasn't going to get married without Lilly in Melio. That had been the deal. That was the arrangement from the beginning.

"There are five hundred important people here." Joelle rose up on her knees. "Grandpapa and Grandmama would be shamed—"

"If Grandpapa can ignore Chantal's misery, then he can learn to ignore his own."

The phone rang, providing momentary distraction. Nic answered the phone, said a quiet yes, and hung up. Things were going to get ugly, Nic thought, taking a deep breath.

"The wedding dress is on its way up."

There was a quiet rap on the door. When Nic opened the door her heart fell. It was the designer from Baraka. She'd personally flown the gown in. A gown that Nic knew she wasn't going to wear today after all.

"*S-salamu alikum.*" *Peace on you,* the designer said, offering the traditional greeting with a deep bow and a smile.

The woman carried the garment bag to Nicolette's bed and laid it flat. "I think you'll like the gown," she said. "The sultan has been most anxious that you approve."

Nic could feel her stomach start to rise. It was like the Danube flooding. She should have talked to Malik this morning, told him she'd meant what she said, asked him to put a stop to the ceremony before it was too late.

But the designer was intent on the task at hand, and she unzipped the garment bag, and drew out a sleek white satin gown with the narrowest shoulder straps imaginable. The gown was cut almost straight across the collarbones, with a very sexy hour glass shape, then flared behind the knees in a long silk train. The train made the dress. The train was hopelessly romantic, a sleek white satin edged with a wide curling ruffle that curved in on itself like icing on a cake.

"Nic," Joelle whispered. "It's like the dress you drew…no sleeves, skinny straps, form fitting curves and not much else."

"No beads, no pearls, no lace, nothing sparkly," Nic recited numbly.

The designer was waiting anxiously for a response. "You're unhappy?"

"No." But Joelle was right, this was the dress she'd sketched on the last night the Ducasse sisters were together, the night before Chantal married Prince Armand. Joelle had been just a teenager, fifteen or sixteen. Chantal had been the mature one at twenty-four. They'd talked about their futures and Chantal had goaded them into drawing their future wedding gowns.

How long ago it seemed. How different things were now compared to then.

"I have to talk to Malik," she choked, queasy, dizzy, unable to let this continue another moment longer. "I have to make a phone call."

Joelle waited, chewing her thumb as Nic dialed Malik's room, but there was no answer. Yet Nic let it ring and ring and ring until the palace switchboard cut in, telling Nic what she already knew—Malik wasn't in his room.

Nic hung up. Stared at the phone, thinking. "Maybe he's already checked into the suite we're using tonight."

"No, he's not." Joelle snapped her fingers. "I completely forgot. He's at the airport meeting the King and Queen of Sweden. They were arriving with members of Spain's royal family and King Nuri thought it'd be nice to welcome them in person."

"Four hours before the wedding?" Panicked, Nic hung the phone up. She had to reach him before this went any further. She couldn't possibly walk down the aisle like this. "Couldn't somebody else do that?"

"Grandpapa was going to go, but King Nuri thought it would be too much for him considering everything that's happening today."

Sensitive of Malik, Nic thought, emotions swinging wildly yet again.

"Your Highness," the designer said, drawing Nicolette's attention, "and this is to hold your veil."

Nic turned around and gaped as the designer presented her with the most magnificent diamond tiara Nic had ever seen.

The tiara was tall, with small fragile arches, and elegant curves and ripples so that the tiara itself seemed to undulate like the desert sands of the Sahara. Within each arch hung a perfect pink tear drop diamond—nine in all—with eight smaller teardrops nestled in the sea of white diamonds below. The arching headband was covered in what looked like a swirling ribbon of miniature pink and white diamonds.

"Incredible," Nic breathed, utterly captivated by the gorgeous pink and white wonder, but with trembling hands she passed the tiara back. "Can't keep it. Far too expensive, obviously an heirloom—"

"It was his mother's. His cousin, Lady Fatima, hand-carried it here today."

"Lady Fatima's here?"

"Indeed. She flew in with her family for the wedding, and brought the crown for you. She'd been keeping it for the sultan's future bride since the sultan's mother died."

Nic turned away, covered her mouth, tried to keep it together. Fatima, who'd waited years for Malik, was here today to lend support.

The designer added with a smile. "Lady Fatima said to remind you that the sultan's beloved must be draped in gold and precious jewels and carried on a table, but that you somehow have managed to miss out on the table."

Nic suddenly laughed, even as tears filled her eyes. Fatima was here. Malik's family was here. How could she not show up? How could she not tell him in advance…just leave him there, in front of five hundred, standing at the altar?

Nic tried to call him over and over during the next three hours but he couldn't be reached, and no one seemed to know anything. Finally it was time to dress and go, or do nothing at all. The moment had come to make a decision.

Joelle stood in Nicolette's room, wearing her pale pink maid of honor gown. She'd been pacing in the hallway until she couldn't bear it anymore and now she was on the verge of tears. "You have to get ready, Nic, or we'll be late. The ceremony begins in thirty minutes."

"I can't—"

"You can! You must." Joelle's eyes welled with tears. "Nic, I don't know what this is about. I don't know if you two had a fight, or you've just got cold feet, but he's been here for you, every step of the way. He cares about you, and I know you love him. It's obvious. It's all over your face."

"I do love him." There was no doubt in her mind about that. "But we weren't ever supposed to be married, we weren't ever supposed to be together. He wanted a different Ducasse—"

"No." Joelle grabbed Nic's wedding dress and shook it in front of her sister. "Maybe he did, maybe he wanted Chantal, but he fell in love with you, so get your dress on and put your tiara on your stubborn blond head and let's go. Because Nic, I know you. You'll never forgive yourself if you hurt him. You love him, and you can't bear to disappoint those that love you, too."

Nic felt an icy shiver rush through her, and goose bumps prickled her skin. That was exactly why she was so upset. Nic had promised Chantal she'd free Lilly. She'd given Chantal her word and it was killing her to let Chantal down. A promise was a promise.

But you also promised Malik. So it must mean it's better to disappoint Malik than Chantal.

"Oh my God." Nic's voice came out broken. "What have I done? What am I doing?" Her chest felt like it was burning up, all ice and heat, all uncontrollable fire. "I do love him. I do and I don't want him standing there, facing everyone, waiting for me."

She blinked and tears fell. "Help me, Joelle. I can't be late."

The distance between the palace and cathedral was less than a mile but it felt like forever to Nic. She was crushed that Chantal and Lilly hadn't come, but she also knew that Malik Nuri was the heart and soul of her future and there was no way she'd stand him up today.

In the back of the chauffeured limousine Joelle squeezed Nic's hand. "Are you okay?"

Nic nodded even though her heart felt like it might explode. Then the car rounded the corner and the Cathedral came into view. Thank God. They'd reached the church with five minutes to spare.

The Cathedral had been built in the Baroque tradition, a lovely domed ceiling painted with a glorious blue and gold vision of heaven complete with angels and all the saints frolicking in eternal joy.

King Remi was waiting for them in the back of the Cathedral. And Nic, who'd been battling for calm, nearly lost her composure when she spotted her grandfather resplendent in his coronation suit, the one he wore for only the most official state business with the purple ribbon and medals of honor.

"Grandpapa," she whispered, leaning forward to kiss him. She smelled the brisk aftershave he'd worn his whole life, a scent old-fashioned and yet elegant, just like him.

His dark eyes filmed with tears. "Tell me you're happy, darling."

She ground her teeth together, knowing she'd walk on fire if she thought it'd give her grandparents peace. They'd been through so much and she knew they were tired. Tired and Worried.

"I'm so happy," she whispered, heart aching, throat sealing closed. Unable to bear so much emotion, Nic impulsively hugged him again, wanting to cling to her childhood for just one more minute. Grandfather Remi to her, King Ducasse to everyone else. "And I'm sorry I spoke sharply to you the other day. I forget you're eighty-five and I'm twenty-seven sometimes."

"You were right." Nic felt her grandfather take a deep shuddering breath. "Your father would never forgive me if I let any of his girls marry, or live, unhappily."

"But I love Malik."

"You should." He drew back, and one of the chapel's dark doors squeaked. A little girl peeked out around the door in a pink silk dress embroidered with great rose-hued flowers.

"Aunt Nicolette?" The soft brown curls, the uncertain smile, the high soft voice of a very young child.

Lilly. "Baby," Nic cried, running toward her niece and swinging her up into her arms. "My little Lilly baby, you're here!"

Lilly's uncertain smile turned positively elfin, the shyness turning into laughter. "I'm not a baby, Aunt Nicolette. I'm four years old. I speak French and Italian and I know how to ski, too."

"You better stop crying," a feminine voice whispered in Nic's ear, even as an arm wrapped around her waist. "You don't want to walk down the aisle with a shiny face."

Chantal. Chantal and Lilly here. Nic couldn't believe it. "What…how…?"

"Grandpapa." Chantal hugged Nic again. "He came for us this morning. He told Phillipe and Catherine they were welcome at the wedding, and he'd like them here, but even if they didn't come, he wanted Lilly and I there." Chantal shrugged. "So here we are."

"Grandpapa did that?"

Chantal nodded. "Well, Malik flew him there, of course. But you already knew that, didn't you?"

No, she didn't, Nic thought, fighting to keep the tears from spilling, but she should have known. Malik was a man of his word.

There was a moment when the organ's triumphant notes filled the glorious fairytale cathedral and the sunlight streamed through the stained-glass windows, and Nic stood at the back of the church, holding her dearest grandfather's arm, seeing her sisters and little Lilly at the front of the church on the left side, and Malik standing on the right, and it was like the moment when she stepped off the yacht in Atiq. Time blurred, lives changed, Nic's senses swam as the past and future came together in a glorious glow of rose, cream and gold.

Nic could smell her flowers—a stunning bouquet of mango calla lilies, conga roses, the most elusive pastel pink tipped cymbidium orchids, and she remembered the way the flower petals had rained down on her head as she stepped off the gangway.

The sun was shining today, just as it had that day, and as the light poured through the high stained-glass window, patterning the guests and floor in bits of blue and gold it was like the domed ceiling of the palace in Baraka. The exotic beauty laden with mystery and promise.

And finally, she could see Malik, her sultan in a long black morning coat, his thick black hair combed back from his handsome face. And when he turned and looked at her from the front of the church it was like the very first moment their eyes met on the harbor wall in Atiq—magic. Just one look and her life would never be the same.

Nic didn't remember walking down the long aisle where each pew was marked with a spray of orchids and rose buds. She didn't remember the prayers, the words spoken, the periodic burst of music, or the cathedral choir. The ceremony was a blur, it was all a strange and haunting beauty, a dream world, she thought, and she didn't wake until Malik lifted her veil and kissed her on her lips.

"Hello, Blondie," he whispered, and he smiled at her, a gorgeous, wicked, sexy smile that melted her all over again. She, who'd never imagined herself marrying, had found true love by pretending to be someone else. Impossible. Incredible. It was an ending plucked straight from a child's storybook.

The reception at the Porto Palace Hotel defied description. Entering the grand ballroom was yet another step into a dream. The sixty three round tables were skirted in luminous pink and purple silk covered by square toppers each hand beaded so the crystals glittered and shone in the candlelight. The pink silk cushions on the chairs were tied with the palest green ribbon, and the flower centerpieces spilled over in a riot of fragrance and color.

Candles shone everywhere—on tables, on pedestals, in gold sconces on the wall—and the cake in the corner was nearly eight feet tall, each one of the nine delectable layers painted different shades of pink and apricot and gold.

She and Malik were inseparable. They ate. They danced. They kissed. They visited with guests. They cut the cake. They danced some more, and this time when dancing, Nicolette knew that she had to be alone with Malik, now. Right now.

"Let's go," she said, linking her fingers with his. "We've been here long enough. Surely we can sneak out?"

He reached up and gently touched her earlobe. "Sneak out?"

Just like that, the words she'd spoken to Chantal four weeks ago, came rushing back. *I'll sneak in, sneak out. He won't even know what's happened.*

It didn't exactly work out that way, did it?

But she and Malik did manage to leave the reception at midnight, exiting quietly through a side door, slipping into one of the royal family's chauffeured cars. At the palace they practically ran up the stairs, and Nicolette was laughing so much by the time she reached the top of the second landing, that she had to lean against one tall marble column, struggling to catch her breath.

Malik reached out with his arms and trapped her against the column. "It's been forever since I've kissed you."

"We kissed yesterday."

"That wasn't a kiss." His lips brushed her cheek, his nose touched her ear and she shivered as his breath caressed her skin. "I want a kiss where I can taste you…everywhere."

The husky note in his voice sent a shot of adrenaline through her. "I think we need a room for that," she answered, grabbing his tie and giving it a tug, pulling him toward their bedroom suite.

Inside their room Malik took control. Despite his own impatience, he wouldn't let them race. He took his time unhooking her snug gown, and with each hook his mouth touched her neck, her back and sometimes he kissed her, and sometimes he licked her and sometimes he bit her, and the wait for the touch became harder to endure.

Her breathing slowed and her belly felt hot and tight with wanting. "It's okay to accelerate things a little," she urged, as his hands became more deliberate, and the wait between bites and licks even longer. She could feel the cool air against her heated skin, feel her breasts swell, aching, her nipples extended begging to be touched and yet he was content kissing a vertebrae in the middle of her back.

But he didn't hurry. His fingers trailed across her skin, making her body burn. She felt feverish by the time her dress spilled open and he pulled her backwards against him, his arms moving around her waist, clasping her, holding her to him. She felt the rigid length of him against the white silk of her panties.

The quiver of her body against his, sent a shudder through him and Nic gulped air as his hands encircled her waist and slowly moved up, shaping her, letting the fullness of her breasts fill his palms and then finding her nipples through the silk of her corset. She whimpered as he pinched the distended nipple. Sensation exploded through her. Hunger, craving, every physical desire.

She was already dissolving against him when his hand slid down her tummy, to the edge of her silk panty, and then lower, finding the heat and moisture between her thighs. She leaned against him, legs disgustingly weak, and the teasing torment of his fingers sinking slowly, deliciously into her creamy heat made her clasp the back of his thighs and hold on to him for dear life. "It's not fair," she choked, struggling to get sound through her throat. "You're still dressed."

"We've time."

"Not that much," she answered breaking away to look up at him through heavy lashes. "I've a wedding and thank you gift to give to you."

Dark color touched his cheekbones. "I don't want gifts."

"But you'll want this." She fought to get control, astonished at the way she responded to him. She felt utterly wild, completely without inhibition. "I want you to undress for me."

He stared at her a long moment and she felt his gaze rest on the full curves of her breast. Her finely boned corset pushed everything up, just barely obscuring the nipples. She could tell he liked her in the corset. He liked her wearing just thigh high stockings and high heels and looking like something from a pinup magazine.

No wonder. He liked hot sex, too. "Your shirt," she commanded.

He watched her face as he started to undress. The shirt came off and she drank him in. His dark hair gleamed, his upper body beautifully bare, the muscles sinewy, arms chiseled like stone.

"Now your belt," she directed coolly. "Then your socks, and trousers."

Silently he unbuckled his belt, slowly drawing it from the loops in his slacks. Her heart began to thud harder, faster as he tossed his belt onto the down-filled chaise. With a lift of his eyebrow, he unzipped his black trousers, letting the material fall open, exposing his taut, flat abdomen with the fine trail of dark hair that disappeared into the low waistband of his silk boxers.

Her mouth went dry. Very dry. Her heart did the craziest somersault. He was hers. Hers. As in forever.

As he stepped from his trousers, she told him to sit down on the bed.

He gave her a sardonic look, but he obeyed, taking a seat on the edge of the mattress, the muscles in his thighs hard, smooth, like the small knots of muscle in his abdomen.

She moved toward him, and putting a hand on each of his knees, she parted his legs to make room for her. Kneeling between his legs, she felt primal, powerful, *female*.

Nic caressed his thighs, felt the muscles bunch beneath her hands.

He reached for her, slid a hand through her long loose hair, turning the blonde strands over, savoring the glossy corn silk color. "You don't have to do anything for me."

"I know. You've made that abundantly clear from the beginning." She caressed the length of his quadriceps again, feeling the warm smooth plane of muscle, and as her light touch slid inward, along the taut muscle of his thigh, she heard him groan. Caressing his thigh again, she explored the width of his chiseled muscle, the shape, the length, the way one muscle wrapped another.

She felt him shudder, saw his erection press against the silk of his boxers, the fabric barely containing him.

Good. He was getting a taste of his own medicine.

Nic caressed him again, this time stroking his belly, his buttocks, the skin beneath his scrotum—anything but his rigid shaft. And when she knew he was reaching the edge of his control, Nic tugged his boxers down and wrapped her hand around the length of him.

"What was that about a kiss isn't a kiss if you can't taste everything...?" she murmured, lowering her head until her long hair fell forward, brushing his naked lap. She heard him swallow yet another groan. Nic brushed her lips across the smooth warm tip of him, and followed the soft kiss with a lick, and she was just about to kiss him again when he slid his fingers through her hair.

"So you've forgiven me then, *laeela?*" His voice came out hoarse. "No hard feelings about getting you here?"

Her hands stroked him, loved him. "Hard feelings about what?"

"Going to Chantal, asking for her help."

Her hands stilled. "I don't understand."

"You love me?"

"Yes."

He titled her chin, looked into her eyes. "I love you. You made me complete today. I feel whole again."

He was saying the right words but there was an undercurrent here that was wrong, and Nic was tired enough, worn down from the wedding and all the stress and nerves that she couldn't put two and two together to make four.

What had Chantal done?

What had Malik done?

Why would Nic need to forgive anyone?

Malik adjusted his boxers, covering himself, and pulled her onto his lap. "Chantal introduced us," he said calmly. "I asked her, too."

"No. You'd proposed to her. You sent her the formal offer—" Nic broke off, a flutter of fear winging through her. She tried to stand. Malik wouldn't let her go.

"Stay here," he said, holding her securely. "We have to talk."

But she'd gone cold, icy cold everywhere. Her arms and legs felt like polished marble. "That letter you sent her," she was struggling to get the words out. Her lips were stiff. Numb. But she managed to stagger to her feet. "You never intended to marry her?"

"No. The letter was essentially my bait."

Bait? She was beginning to understand how it'd worked. It'd been a con. The letter had been a *con.* Nic took a step away, not knowing where to go, what to think. Chantal hadn't truly set her up, had she? Chantal and Malik couldn't have set this whole charade up, could they? "You never wanted my sister."

"You're the one—and the only one—I've ever wanted."

CHAPTER FOURTEEN

STANDING there in her strapless silk corset and her insubstantial thigh high white hose, Nic saw how ridiculous she looked. How ridiculous she must have looked for the past three weeks.

He'd known she was Nicolette from the moment the yacht docked at his harbor wall. He'd known the only Ducasse coming to Atiq would be Nicolette. There had never been any other Ducasse princess...just a plan to force Nicolette to the altar and fill the Ducasse coffers.

The icy cold in her face gave way to a burning heat. She was blushing now, embarrassed. Ashamed. Here she'd been feeling so noble. She'd felt so good about her decisions...her compromises. Her *sacrifices*. She was giving up her own best interests for the sake of Lilly and Chantal's happiness.

But now she saw it was just a big joke. She'd been set up. *Set up*. How could Chantal do this? Chantal wasn't a trickster. Chantal wasn't cunning and manipulative. How could she sell her own sister out?

"You're angry," Malik said, lying on his bed, the sheet low on his hip, watching her fume and pace.

"Damn straight." Nic stared at him through new eyes. He was a schemer. A player. A playboy.

Oh God, she'd married just what she'd sworn she'd always avoid.

"She did it to help you," he said, arms folded behind his head now.

Shut up, she wanted to tell him. "Marriage doesn't help me."

"It helps your country." Because Melio gets money, a serious investor and developer, as well as a strong arm to keep bullying neighbors at bay. "She said you'd all agreed to marriages that would improve your country's situation, and position," he continued remorselessly.

Nic couldn't listen to this. They'd both tricked her. They'd

172

both known she hadn't ever wanted to marry but they'd ignored what she wanted, what she'd believed, and forced their own wishes on her. "Did she come to you, or you go to her?"

He smiled, as if finding her question touching. "Trying to figure out who's the villain?"

"You're both the villain," she retorted grimly, "but yes, I'd like to know who initiated this…sham of a marriage."

His expression grew dark. "It's not a sham. It's a real marriage. Legal. Consummated. Permanent."

"You haven't answered my question."

He shrugged, as if the answer was obvious. "I went to her. After I went to your grandfather."

Her lips parted. "You went to Grandfather? In the very beginning?"

"Of course. He is the King. No one else could give me permission to marry you, and all it would take is his permission."

Ridiculous! "What about *my* permission? What about my free will?" It stunned her to think that Grandpapa could be in on this, too. It was as if the entire kingdom wanted Nicolette settled, married, belly fat with baby.

He patted the bed. "You came to Baraka of your own free will."

"Because I thought I could go! I thought a couple weeks as a brunette, a few state dinners, and then voila, off to Baton Rouge, see Chantal and Lilly safe, and then I'd be back to Melio, back to blonde, back to life as I prefer it."

"You're shivering. There's no reason to let yourself get so worked up." He sat up, pushed the covers aside. "Come back to bed, *laeela*."

She couldn't even look at him. All those comments he'd made about her sister "Nicolette," those remarks about her beautiful brown hair, the digs against blondes. He'd been having a grand time, hadn't he? He'd really enjoyed himself, and he'd planned it all. Every little bit of it. "I can't."

"You can." His voice dropped. "You will."

"You can't boss me around. I never let you before, and I'm certainly not about to start now." She was shivering, she realized, seeing how goose bumps covered her arms. She needed to get dressed. "I can't believe what a fool I was. Such a romantic idiot."

"Nothing's changed."

"Nothing?" she sputtered, turning to face him, eyes wide with shock. How could he say nothing had changed? Their whole relationship was…a lie! "I don't even know you, Malik Nuri. I thought…I thought…"

"You thought what? That I was a fool, that I was just another man you'd lead around like a little spoiled poodle?"

"I've never treated a man like that!"

"You've treated every man like that. You use your beauty against men. You dazzle them, you win them, you dump them. I wanted you, and I was willing to take some risks to woo you. You can't be angry because I beat you at your own game."

Damning words, she thought, fighting tears. But he was right, of course. She was furious with him—and herself—for precisely that reason. She'd thought she could pull the charade off—and she'd expected to escape from her charade relatively unscathed. Instead she was married. Instead she'd be spending the rest of her life in Baraka.

"You were so dishonest." She sputtered the words, riding an endless roller coaster of emotion. She was married, *married,* and it was all a…trick. He'd set her up and then tricked her…coerced her…into marrying him, knowing perfectly well her fear of commitment. He'd found a way to get her to the altar and more.

"You weren't honest, either," he answered calmly, completely unruffled by her furious outburst, "and I never blamed you. I knew you. Understood you. You're competitive. You like to win."

"This isn't about winning."

"*Laeela,* it's only about winning."

She couldn't even see straight. "Yes, but two wrongs don't make a right!"

"I'd planned to tell you the truth."

"When?" she demanded, marching toward the bed. "Because I don't remember you coming clean, either."

"No, I didn't confess. I figured I'd tell you, when you told me. But you didn't. So I didn't." He smiled like a cat with a big bowl of cream. "Nic, darling, you wanted me. You have me. Forever."

He really didn't need to add that last part, she thought bitterly, wanting to grab a pillow and cover his smiling face. "But I didn't *want* to be married."

"But if you're going to be married, aren't you glad you married me?"

"So not the point, Your Royal Highness."

"Some points become pointless." His massive shoulders shrugged carelessly. He'd become the ultimate male, all contented authority. "We are married, and we're going to enjoy our life together. We certainly enjoy each other."

"Not anymore," she flashed, turning away, unable to stomach this a moment longer. This whole time, all these weeks…the night she'd spent in his arms…

"What was my bride price?" she whispered, her gaze on the sparkling lights of the port. It was quiet now, but if she hadn't married Malik, it could have been jammed with cruise ships and passengers, the very thing the Ducasse family had been desperate to avoid.

He didn't leave the bed. "High."

She swallowed hard. "How high?"

"Twenty-five."

"Twenty-five…?"

"Million."

"Dollars?" she choked, turning around, staring at him incredulously. "Tell me that's not dollars."

"It's not dollars. It's pounds. My bank in London handled the transaction."

Nic slowly sat down on the window sill. The glass felt cool against her nearly bare back. The wire in the silk bustier pressed against her underarms. "That's it?" she jested, feeling absolutely flattened. She'd been an extremely expensive wife. Not to mention extremely reluctant.

"Another twenty-five million when our first child turns fifteen."

She couldn't take this in. She couldn't believe anyone would spend that kind of money…even if one wanted a royal wife. "Why fifteen?" she asked, giving up on even keeping the facts straight.

"At fifteen, our son or daughter could legally assume the throne, without need of a guardian. That's important. Guardians often attempt to seize control. So fifteen is important."

She felt her eyes burn. Carefully she drew a breath, refusing to let even one tear form. "Are you planning on going somewhere in fifteen years?"

"No."

"I see." But she didn't see. She didn't understand anything right now. Standing, Nic glanced around for a robe, something to wrap around her now that she'd grown cold. Instead she picked up her discarded wedding gown. Stepping into the slim skirt, she fought to keep her tears from falling. What a terrible end of a beautiful day.

"Errands?" he asked quietly, his tone losing all playfulness.

She swallowed the tears. She didn't care if he was watching her, looking at her with that combination of worry and understanding. He could pretend he understood her. He could pretend he cared.

She hiccupped, stuck her arms through the thin straps and held the back of her dress together with one hand. "I think I'd prefer sleeping alone tonight."

"There's no reason to do this—"

"There is," she interrupted fiercely. But she ruined her defiance by letting her lower lip quiver. "I'm hurt. And angry. I'm going to go to my old room. I need to be alone."

"Why?"

"I have to think."

Malik slowly rose, wearing nothing but his boxer shorts. "You'll just get angrier."

"Probably."

"But if it's what you want…?"

"It is."

He didn't approach her, didn't kiss her. Instead he headed for the bathroom. "Good night."

The worst wedding night in history, Nicolette told herself for the hundredth time, fighting tears all night long. She couldn't sleep and she couldn't rest and yet she was too tired to get up and actually do anything, either.

But morning did arrive and Nic dragged herself into the shower, and then put on a least-likely-to-be-a-princess outfit—ratty jeans and a super soft pink cotton T-shirt. The pink reminded her of her gorgeous floral bouquet from yesterday, and her eyes stung.

This was all her fault.

Well, Chantal and Malik's, too.

Chantal entered Nic's room while Nicolette was sliding her feet into a pair of leather loafers.

"One of the housemaids said you'd slept here last night," Chantal said, glancing at Nic's bed, the sheets tossed on only one side of the bed. "You slept alone?"

"Glad the housemaids are keeping everyone informed," Nic answered, standing. She was *not* in the mood to talk. Her heart hurt. She felt…used.

Chantal sat down in the armchair near the window, gracefully crossing her legs. "I'm sorry, Nic."

Nic looked away, fighting the angry words that came to her lips. She didn't want to fight with Chantal, not when Chantal was still so ecstatic about getting Lilly free from Armand's family in La Croix. It was the first time Lilly had been away from La Croix in nearly two years. And now that she was home here in the palace, Lilly would be safe.

"You should have told me." Nic's voice came out husky.

"It was a bit underhanded—"

"A bit?"

Chantal blushed. "But I knew you'd like him, Nic. I know your type. I just wanted you two to meet. I thought you'd hit it off, and you did. And I knew you wouldn't marry him unless you wanted to."

Nic exhaled in a rush. "We agreed you'd never play matchmaker with me."

"But stop for a minute and think about the big picture," Chantal said, moving toward the door. "You haven't just saved one country, you've saved two. Melio needed King Nuri's money, but King Nuri needed you."

King Nuri did not need her, Nic fumed, leaving her bedroom, heading outside. King Nuri wanted a royal marriage, and heirs—don't forget the heirs—but he didn't need *her*. In this instance, any fertile princess would surely do.

She set off for the water, cutting through the extensive palace grounds, zig zagging through the rose garden, the perennial garden, the formal maze, the little rock garden with the imported alpine flowers that one royal from Salzburg had planted in hopes of bringing a little bit of Austria to her new home.

But Nic didn't pay attention to any of the glorious flowers or the pale morning sunlight glinting off the water. She was thinking of Malik and his trickery, thinking of Chantal who had trapped her into marriage—two people she respected, two people she trusted.

She couldn't believe it.

Couldn't understand it.

Why not just introduce her and Malik at a party, say, "Nicolette, this is King Nuri, sultan of Baraka, and I thought you two would hit it off together…"

Nic kicked a pebble, watched it bounce, and on reaching it, kicked it a second time, this kick sending it flying so high and far that it disappeared over the stone wall into the port itself.

"Nice kick," a male voice drawled.

Nic turned around and spotted a man in jeans and a thin cashmere turtleneck sweater leaning against the wall behind them. She sized him up, saw that he was young and fit, and from the way the sweater clung to his biceps, obviously quite muscular. "I used to play football," she said irritably.

"I bet you were good."

"Very good." She was so mad, so mad at people—and men—that she had no desire to be nice to anyone. "Enjoy the sunshine," she said, eager to move on.

But his voice stopped her. "It must feel pretty wonderful bringing a man back to life."

What was that? Nic turned, looked at the stranger, a scathing retort on her lips when she realized that this man spoke like Malik, same kind of rich, cultured tone, same husky pitched voice except his accent was more English, more uppercrust, less…desert.

He was dark like Malik, too, but his eyes were golden—amber—and his expression was harder, more cynical. He might be wearing jeans but he was already an old soul. Jaded.

He drew on his cigarette, held the air in, turned the cigarette to look at the burning tip and then exhaling, dropped the cigarette and crushed it out. "I take it he didn't tell you about the—attempt?"

"Who?"

JANE PORTER   179

His eyebrows lifted, satirical. "King Malik Roman Nuri."

And she suddenly put it all together. "You're a cousin or..."

"The younger brother."

Kalen, she silently said, understanding. "You came for the wedding."

He laughed. "I was the best man."

"I didn't—"

"See me. I know. You only had eyes for my brother." He looked at her for a long moment. "Congratulations on the wedding. I guess that makes us family."

She nodded, crossed her arms over her chest, still angry, still hurt. "What did you mean by the 'attempt'?"

"The assassination attempt." His golden gaze met hers. "Last year."

It seemed there were many important things Malik hadn't told her. Nic put a hand to her stomach, feeling sick. Somebody had tried to hurt Malik.

Her Malik?

"He hushed it up," Kalen continued calmly, as if his news were inconsequential. "Baraka's secret service agents arrested the shooter and Malik acted as if nothing had happened. But something had. Obviously. He wasn't the same afterward."

Kalen's jaw grew tight, and for the first time Nicolette saw how Kalen's cavalier attitude hid his deep family ties. "There was a time I almost thought I'd have to return to Atiq. Put on the old *jellaba* again," he continued lightly, but his golden gaze was hard and angry. "He'll never tell you, but the attempt killed something in him, stole his spirit. And then he realized that he had to provide for his country. It was his duty."

Duty, she silently echoed, hearing Malik's voice in her head and one of their many, endless conversations about duty and choice, responsibility...

She took several steps away, leaned on the low stone wall overlooking the water. "He wasn't going to tell me."

"Probably not," Kalen answered calmly. "He's a king."

Nic felt the roughness of the wall bite into her knuckles. He was a King. He was also a man. A very great man. Her chest squeezed. Malik should have told her so many damn things. She pushed off the wall, furious all over again. "I better go back."

Kalen's dark head inclined. "He'll be worried about you."

Nic felt a rush of pain, and just like that Kalen had diffused her anger. How had Kalen managed to find the chink in her armor so quickly? She loved Malik. She'd never want Malik to worry—especially not about her. She never wanted to add to his burden, create more stress in his life. She wanted to help him. Protect him.

Love him.

She shook her head, struggling to smile but couldn't. Her heart had never felt so bruised. Less than three weeks ago she'd met Malik for the first time. Now she couldn't imagine her life without him. "Will we see you again before you return to London?"

"I doubt it." His smile gentled. *"Allah ihennik."*

"May God's peace go with you, too, Prince Kalen."

Nic started off, back up the stone path leading to the palace gardens.

"Queen Nuri—" Kalen called out.

She stopped, glanced over her shoulder and saw that Kalen still leaned against the low stone wall.

"I don't know what he told you, but he loves blondes." Kalen's teeth flashed white. "He'd never marry a brunette."

Nic waved farewell, bit back a smile. The Nuris were impossible. How could she have married into this family? How could she possibly have agreed to marry *anyone* after only three weeks?

Climbing the palace staircase, she headed for the elegant guest suite which had been given to them as a bridal suite. The door was unlocked and Nic walked in, through the grand entry, the elegant sitting room and into the bedroom where Malik was still in bed.

Enjoying breakfast in bed.

Nic dropped into a chair opposite the bed. "Bastard."

He looked up from the newspaper he was reading in bed. He was wearing a scholarly pair of glasses and a tray with freshly baked croissants, juice and coffee sat next to him in bed. "Good morning, wife."

"You're right. I don't like losing. I thought…"

"You could win," he concluded, pulling his reading glasses off. "But you did win. You got me. And you know I love you."

"And you know I was terrified of marriage." She balled her

hands. "So far, my early impressions of marriage aren't positive, either."

He smiled sympathetically which was the wrong thing to do. "It's not funny, Malik. You don't just manipulate women into marriage."

"Let alone extremely popular, eligible princesses."

"Let alone," she agreed hotly.

"I wanted you."

"But life doesn't work like that."

"It does. If you find your soul mate."

She crossed her legs, shook her head, thinking he was so unbelievably confident. "But you'd be honest with your *soul mate*," she answered, her voice growing husky. "You'd tell her the truth—"

"Just like you told me the truth?" He set his paper aside. "Come on, Nic, this isn't about honesty. It's about power. Control. You're angry because you were outsmarted."

"You didn't outsmart me."

"I did. You're just a sore loser." He pushed the covers away and climbed from the bed. "I detest sore losers."

He was naked. Beautifully naked.

"You're cheating," she whispered, "you can't walk around naked when we're fighting."

He ignored her, pulling her to her feet, closing the distance between them. She sighed as his hands slid around her waist, moving to the small of her back and then lower, to clasp her backside. "You're still cheating," she gasped, as his hands continued a very slow, thorough caress across her bottom.

"I've never met anyone so obsessed with winning." He kissed the side of her neck, then lifted her long hair and kissed the pale skin at her nape. "But all's fair in love and war. And you have to know, *laeela*, I'd do anything to keep you from running."

"But why, Malik? And why me?"

His hands stilled on her hips. He stared down at her, his expression unusually fierce. "I've become a realist. I'm driven by practicality. And although I knew you weren't interested in marriage, I admired your independence. You didn't see marriage as a means of getting things. You wanted a relationship where you were an equal—"

"Yes, and yet what did you do? You trapped me into marriage, you live in a country where women aren't equal—"

"And I know if anything happens to me you will stand by our children no matter what," he interrupted. "I can imagine no other woman as the mother of my children. I chose you, not based on beauty or title, but out of respect."

Nic's eyes burned, so hot and scalding she had to look away. "Surely there were better suited women in Baraka."

"I needed a wife who wouldn't be intimidated by power or politics. You're not just a princess that understands duty, you've studied math and science, you've traveled extensively. And best of all, you embraced my country and our customs."

She hated the lump filling her throat. She struggled to swallow, lifting her chin as she did so. "There was an assassination attempt last year."

He looked at her strangely. "No one knows."

"Your family knows."

His eyes narrowed. He considered her for a long moment. "Kalen had no right."

Damn these arrogant men! It didn't matter if they were a sultan or a king, they were all the same. All they ever thought about was their reputation. "He loves you." She glared at him. "Although why, I don't know."

He reached out to her, clasped her face between his hands. "I've waited years to marry. I didn't think I'd ever find anyone right for me—but you are right for me, and I know in my soul, where my hope and my ancestors live, that you are the only one for me."

She pushed against his chest, feeling the smooth hard muscle beneath her fists. His skin was warm and fragrant. His nearness was doing crazy things to her senses. "Do you have any idea how much I love you? Do you have any idea how much your life means to me?" She heard the catch in her voice, felt the heartbreak on the inside. Knowing his family history, knowing how his grandfather had died must add to his fear.

"I don't want anyone to hurt you," she whispered, knowing the burden he carried, understanding even better the great love and compassion he felt for his people. "I don't want anyone to take you from me."

"I don't want anyone to take me from you, either, but if the unthinkable should happen, *laeela,* I know you will be a tiger in the palace. You will fight like hell for our children. You will do whatever is necessary to protect them—''

''But nothing is going to happen to you.'' She wrapped her arms around his waist, burying her face against his chest. ''I'm not going to let anything happen to you. For better or worse, you are my other half and if you're going to give me children then you have an obligation to stick around and help raise them. Understand?''

''Is that an order?''

''It's the first edict from Nicolette Nuri, Queen of Baraka.''

He laughed softly, and lifting her chin, he studied her as the morning sunshine illuminated her face. ''Yes, my beloved Nicolette.'' He dipped his head, kissed her deeply, thoroughly. On lifting his head, he gave her a little wicked smile. ''And now, Queen Nuri, your husband, the King, and Sultan of Baraka requests that your clothes come off. The King wants you naked and kneeling in his bed.''

''Naked and *kneeling?*'' She balked indignantly. ''Well you can tell your King—'' she broke off, and despite blushing wildly, her curiosity got the better of her. ''Why does he want me kneeling?''

Malik was trying desperately hard not to laugh. ''There are still a couple choice positions for the royal newlyweds to try, including the King's personal favorite, Catch the Tiger.''

Nic didn't know whether to be amused or mortified. ''I certainly hope it's nothing to do with the tiger's tail.''

''Most definitely not. The King wouldn't want to harm your tail. You have a beautiful tail.'' And kissing her again he reached for the hem of her pink T-shirt and tugged it over her head. ''And never forget, you have free will. You can stop me anytime.''

Stop him? Nic thought, hearing the zipper on her jeans go, and swoosh as the faded denim came down over her hips. *Not a snowball's chance in hell.*

EPILOGUE

THE fire glowed on the soft red sandstone walls. The Citadel had always been so beautiful and mysterious at night, and Nicolette watched four-year-old Zaid's face, the boy's big green eyes impossibly wide as Malik threw another log on the fire and hot orange sparks shot up into the dark sky.

Malik was telling tales now, stories of the boys' brave Barakan ancestors, of the battles once won and lost here in the dramatic mountains. Sitting on the red wool carpet, Nic felt little Aden press his face against her middle, his heart pounding like mad through his two-year-old chest, and she shot Malik an exasperated glance. Her husband was nearly as bad as the children. He loved bringing the children to Zefd, loved these nights when they sat out by the fire and they pretended to be nomads and Bedouin instead of a powerful king and his sons.

"You're scaring them," she whispered to Malik over the little boys' heads.

"It's a campfire. We're telling campfire stories."

"They're still just little boys."

His brow furrowed and he shot a protective glance at Zaid and then Aden who peeped up at his father from beneath his mother's arm. "Should I stop?" he asked the children.

"No, no," cried Zaid, and of course little Aden chimed in, trying to copy his brother, wanting to be brave like Zaid.

Nic groaned to herself. Malik knew better than to ask the children, but then, men were men and they never changed. Yet she didn't really want him to change, either. She loved him so much, and she loved to see Malik like this—so relaxed, so happy here in Zefd. When they were here at the Citadel, together like this, Malik's cares seemed to melt away and right now, Malik looked nearly as young and carefree as the boys.

He needed the break, she thought, heart softening. They

184

should have made this trip months ago. But at least they were here now, and Malik was making up for lost time with his boys.

Nicolette knew she'd done many good things in her life, but nothing was better than making the children. The children had made her and Malik's lives complete.

Nic ran her hand across Aden's small head. His black hair was still silky, the long loose curls nearly reaching his shoulders. Someday the curls would be cut. The baby would grow up.

Please don't let time pass too quickly, she said in a silent prayer. Let time slow. Let us stay together for as long as we can.

Malik caught her gaze. He felt the wash of her intense devotion. ''You love your boys.''

Her chest suffused with bittersweet warmth. ''I do. All of them.''

A log rolled over, shooting up another stream of sparks, and Nic thought back to the past five years, and she knew she'd change nothing about them, and nothing about their marriage. Malik was perfect for her: the right combination of strength, integrity and sensuality. He kept her on her toes. He never let life get boring. And best of all, he'd taught her that sometimes one has to lose, to win.

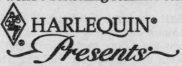

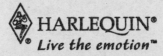

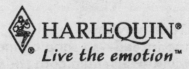

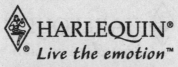

The world's bestselling romance series.

Seduction and Passion Guaranteed!

THE PRINCESS BRIDES

For duty, for money...for passion!

Discover a thrilling new trilogy from a rising star of Harlequin Presents®, Jane Porter!

Meet the Royals...

Chantal, Nicolette and Joelle are members of the blue-blooded Ducasse family. Step inside their sophisticated and glamorous world and watch as these beautiful princesses find they have to marry three international playboys—for duty, for money... and definitely for passion!

Don't miss

THE SULTAN'S BOUGHT BRIDE (#2418)
September 2004

THE GREEK'S ROYAL MISTRESS (#2424)
October 2004

THE ITALIAN'S VIRGIN PRINCESS (#2430)
November 2004

Pick up a Harlequin Presents® novel and you will enter a world of spine-tingling passion and provocative, tantalizing romance!

Available wherever Harlequin books are sold.

www.eHarlequin.com

HPPBJPOR